We Go Camping

by

Adrian Whyles

Published by New Generation Publishing in 2023

First Edition

ISBN   978-1-80369-690-4

www.newgeneration-publishing.com
 New Generation Publishing

For those who are special in my life:

Sharon

Rhiannon

Bethany

Sam

Penelope

And thanks Richard for the cover artwork. A talent I can only dream of.

CHAPTER ONE

Mindful that Jo had always been quite a sensitive child, John let the subject drop; the rest of the journey to college lacked conversation, with only the sound of music to fill the void.

The subject was Jo and her mother moving to Spain to live. This had come as quite a shock the previous evening when Jo had sat her father down and delivered the news in a very nervous and emotional manner.

"I think it will be good for me to experience another culture, and I will learn another language, and it will broaden my knowledge, and it will help my studying, and just be really good for me," she said in one big flurry of words, which she had obviously rehearsed, but didn't sound as reasoned to her as when she practiced it.

"It doesn't mean I don't love you, or want to see you." Her voice had now started to quiver, and her eyes were about to brim over with the tears that had formed. "And mum says I will still be able to come back and stay with you quite a lot. I wouldn't go if I couldn't do that."

The "love you" part had made John well-up a bit, as it always did. But this was a different 'welling-up'. Not the one that happens when you've just heard "I love you"—the best thing you could ever hear from your child, making you feel so happy, but the one that occurs when you know it's going to be a sad ending.

Whilst Jo was talking, John experienced about five emotions in an equal number of minutes. Sadness, anger, self-pity, loneliness and then back to anger. He didn't want to be angry with her, but he had had no warning that this was coming. He felt he should discuss the matter in more detail with Jo's mother, as it seemed that his feelings had not been taken into consideration.

So, out came the spur of the moment, aggressive question, which had been delivered with a raised voice, making it a 'battle' from the start.

"How the hell long have you been organising this with your mother behind my back, and not felt the need to mention this 'minor' change to life?"

Whilst John thought he had a point, his tactless approach had put Jo on the defensive from the start.

"I did not do this behind your back," she said, sharply. Tears now welling over.

John managed to regain his composure, but there were questions that still needed answering. It wouldn't wait until morning, either, whereby a more reasoned conversation could take place. He wanted answers now.

Silence ensued. Jo staring at the floor, sniffing occasionally, and wiping her eyes a couple of times. John composing himself. Then, after a few minutes, he began

"Okay, when did you start to talk about this?"

The answer alarmed him.

"Mum asked me a few months ago. When I was with her over New Year."

"Jesus!" John yelled. "Five bloody months you've been planning this! When are you going?"

"It's not definite yet" she said. "And certainly not until college has finished in July."

"Where are you going to live?"

"Mum's been looking into southern Spain, but away from any holiday resorts."

Obviously, her mother's trip to Spain at Easter was more than just a holiday, he thought.

And so the questions continued. At times it turned into an emotional minefield, and generally, the atmosphere remained on a knife edge. Jo was very upset and knew her dad was unhappy. So she kept trying to reassure him, but this whole thing was ripping John apart, and he needed Jo to be in bed, so he could try and come to terms with what he regarded right now, as the worst possible thing that could happen to him.

As he sat alone, the house silent, it brought guilt to the surface, another emotion which John had felt from time to time, since the divorce. Jo had had to deal with it since she was nine. She had shown amazing strength dealing with her world 'falling apart'. What right had he got to make her feel as though she were letting him down? None whatsoever, he thought. But why not talk to me about it? Does she not feel she can talk to me? Am I an unreasonable angry person? He knew the answer to that one…. "At times, yes!"

He wanted to take his anger out on something, but his sensible head took control. He was very upset, and then angry, then upset again, and so it went on, well into the night. By the time he wearily climbed into bed, he only had a couple of hours before he needed to be awake so that he could listen to make sure Jo was up and entering the bathroom for her obligatory forty-five minute occupation. He had decided that he didn't want the journey to Jo's college to have an awkward silence, so he would let her know that he'd accepted her decision, she could move on with his blessing, and he would emphasise how much he loved her, and just how much he was going to miss her.

And that theory was perfect. However, in practice he found it a little more difficult to keep the anger at a manageable level. The journey was only a short distance, which probably did them both a favour. John's determination to stay calm was not proving successful.

Jo was a bright kid, no question about it. Everyone says that about their own, but her SATs and GCSEs had proved it. A's were common place throughout course work and exams, so Jo had applied herself faultlessly. John and her mother's divorce, still played on John's mind from time to time, but Jo had coped well, certainly outwardly, and they had maintained a great relationship, which was so important to John. He had supported financially, as he should, and he was thankful to his successful sales consultancy business which continued to allow him to provide. As it was his own business, it also had allowed him to be relatively flexible, and spend extra time with Jo, outside of the agreed one night in the week and every other weekend. Of course, this was all about to change. "Only a few times a year, at best," he had said to himself during one of his upset stages, late last night.

So, instead of the calculated soft agreeable approach, John came straight out with, "You know that seeing me regularly isn't really going to happen is it? It will be a few times a year at best."

"No, I told mum it has to be every month, and she said that would be fine with her."

"That will be fine with her if I pay for the flights every time," John responded curtly "You'd better get used to the fact that we will see a lot less of each other, and that's why I'm so upset about it."

Like she wasn't. And that's what stopped the conversation in the car. Jo's head dropped, and John could tell tears were falling. He turned the music up slightly in a brief attempt to diffuse the situation; they had a common love of music, not necessarily all the same taste, but it often brought them together if relations had been a little strained. But he couldn't think of what to say, and Jo obviously realised that "every month" probably was a bit ambitious.

They arrived at college. Jo picked up her bag slowly, trying to think of what to say, but John broke the uneasy silence that existed between them: "I love you, and I'm going to miss you. I'm angry and sad at the same time."

"I know, and I love you, too," she said.

John couldn't help himself: "But you won't miss me so much, because it'll be warm, sunny and much better than here." A misplaced attempt at a joke, if ever there was one.

Jo said nothing; she looked away and got out of the car, slamming the door closed behind her.

John watched her walk away, realising that hadn't finished well.

"Shit!" He exclaimed out loud, and hit the steering wheel with both hands. "Dickhead!" Angry with himself, he drove away and headed home, playing the music very loud.

Working the business from home with no one to meet with, face to face, had its advantages. Today was a prime example. John couldn't think of anything else but Jo's move. Work was not really front of mind. He knew he would have to speak to Jo's mother, and that he might get angry. So he decided to leave it for a few days. It was Friday, he didn't have Jo this weekend, and he could have a couple of beers down his local with the lads, and they would help him put things into perspective.

"Clearly, this whole episode is sending you delusional," he said to himself. What on earth made him believe for one moment that either Morris, Gary or Eddie would help him 'put things into perspective'? They were each capable of showing emotion if the pub shut for a day, but to think they would be of any comfort at a time like this was optimistic at best. However, distraction was what he needed, and they would certainly provide that.

John felt quite lonely for the rest of the day, even though he had managed to put together a couple of reports, send them off, and speak to one or two prospective clients. His patience level wasn't quite at its peak, but he completed the day without major incident, and had arranged to meet the guys as usual that evening.

Other than when he had Jo staying, John's time was his own. He hadn't had a partner for some time, and wasn't particularly looking for one. His only other distraction was golf. He didn't play much of that, either. His consultancy business was earning him a decent living, but had taken a few years to build up. He was only 21 when Jo was born, so money had initially been tight. He now considered himself to be at a stage where he could enjoy his times with Jo, and also enjoy other pursuits. Problem was, he always found himself working too many hours, hence the lack of any other pursuits. But he had decided to do something about it, and Jo moving was going to force his hand or else he really would have little to look forward to.

So he set off on the twenty-minute walk to the pub, still turning things over in his mind. Should he tell the guys just yet? After all, he didn't really know too much of the detail, and if they asked questions, he might not know the answers. Wouldn't that make it seem like he wasn't too bothered, having not demanded the detail? Actually, now he thought about it, he wondered whether or not this was a permanent move?

Best to gather some other viewpoints. The guys may not be the most sensitive people in the world, but for all their irrelevant comments, there might be one or two that make sense. John smiled to himself. If he had to put money on who would show an ounce of understanding, who would it be?

Morris? Odds marginal. John didn't know too much of Morris's background, only that he had moved from Wales to the Reading area thirteen years ago. It was as close to London as "I can afford", was Morris's explanation. John had met him and Eddie in the pub a few years previous, and they both had a different outlook on life, which John found quite amusing. Morris could be considered to be a bit of a loner, because he never spoke of any other friends or family. He was proud to be Welsh, but had never returned to his homeland since the day he left. He would not refer to his occupation as anything other than "a waste collection manager", and was upset by the term 'Dustbin man'. He earned enough money to pay for his small flat, eating mostly junk food, and having a drink down the pub.

"Where do you see yourself in ten years' time?" John once asked during a boozy philosophical night in the pub.

Morris pondered for a few seconds, before replying in his very faint Welsh accent, "Down here I suppose, but obviously a little wiser." Wiser about what was anybody's guess. If John had brought The Telegraph to the pub during lunch time, Morris would stand by his claim that his tabloid newspaper had the same news in it, just not in "the same fancy words". His other strange 'quirk' was that he never shaved during the week, apart from Friday and Saturday. He would on those days in case he met the woman of his dreams, despite the fact that he never ventured anywhere further than the pub.

"You won't take the piss when one night she walks in here," Morris said. "Then who will be laughing." The others were quite happy to let Morris believe that the woman of his dreams would decide to come looking for him in the pub.

Eddie? If the odds were marginal with Morris, they were heavily stacked against, in terms of any compassion coming from Eddie. Although he had just turned forty, he still lived at home with his mum. On the first occasion of meeting Eddie's mother, she had asked John to employ him. "Can't you find him something to do, so he can earn a salary, afford his own place and leave me alone!" she exclaimed.

Eddie's father had left when Eddie was only five years old. "I'm the man of the house, and I've always seen it as my responsibility to support and protect my mother," he always claimed. Free board and lodgings was probably nearer the truth in his current circumstances. Eddie lived on benefits, but he was always available to help Morris and his "band of merry men" if they were a man down on a particular day, or covered holidays. Strictly cash only, and he did pass some of that on to his mother. He never really took himself, or the world, very seriously. But his belief that the better off should "support", as he called it, the less better off, often wound others up to the point of the subject needing to be changed before somebody said something they might regret. Eddie, on the other hand, would never say anything he would later regret. He didn't seem to care too much about anything. John always felt Eddie was letting life pass him by, and stated this on a number of occasions, but it fell on deaf ears. Eddie wasn't going to change, that had become quite apparent.

Eddie did have a sense of humour, which made the others smile quite regularly. Conversations about current affairs would always draw opinions from Eddie. They would put a completely different angle on whatever topic was being discussed, and sometimes the theory was difficult to follow, but there was usually an amusing connotation. A prime example being when they were discussing the fate of Tiger Woods, and his knee injury. Eddie was convinced it was an insurance scam, despite admitting that the man was so wealthy, he didn't need to do that. They quickly moved on to another subject. He did always seem to make women laugh too.

"They're laughing at you, though" Gary once told him.

"No, I think you'll find women bring out my true personality, and we connect." Once again, the subject was not pursued.

Gary? Probably the best chance John had of receiving anything like understanding, although he wouldn't put a lot of money on it. Gary was thirty-seven and they had known each other for about ten years when the two met in the music store Gary worked in. John was a regular visitor, and over a period of time they connected on their favourite subject, and their friendship grew. Gary since left the store, or was sacked, it wasn't quite clear, and Gary was always a bit vague. He sold CDs and DVDs on line and at fairs, but was never keen to talk about his suppliers.

As a single person, Gary fancied himself a bit with the girls, hence his slight annoyance that Eddie seemed to be more successful at gaining their attention. He liked a drink with the lads, and had a relatively gentle demeanour. His business seemed to be thriving, so however he was running it, John thought best to leave well alone. To the best of John's knowledge, he had only had one relationship in the last ten years (which had lasted a year or so), but Gary couldn't be faulted for his attempts. "I can't find one that understands my business ethics," was his assessment of the situation. John was more of the opinion that, since Gary seemed to lack any business ethics, no female was prepared to accept a relationship where their partner did not allow questions regarding business and its legality.

So there he had it. On reflection, three mates he was about to spend the evening with, who in their individual ways were entertaining, and good company, so perhaps they were exactly what he needed right now.

As he arrived at the pub, he could see through the window that Morris and Eddie were already there (arrive before the others was always Eddie's policy, so that he could boast of always being first to buy a round – but actually arriving early, so as to avoid a 'full' round). It was no great surprise that the two of them were just finishing their first pints as John entered.

"Perfect timing," Eddie exclaimed as he downed the final mouthful when John greeted them.

"Funny that," John said. "That's never happened before."

He made his way to the bar. He would have to make a special effort to be tolerant this evening. He felt that perhaps his patience or humour wasn't going to be at its best, because what had just happened, never usually bothered him. In fact, Morris and Eddie's consistency amused him normally, but just then he had found it slightly annoying. "Don't rise to it this evening," he told himself, as he paid for the three pints.

"A bag of nuts each, and one for yourself," Eddie called out. John looked down at the bar and smiled. He decided that a few pints were definitely needed this evening.

CHAPTER TWO

Moments later Gary arrived, and it wasn't long before the four of them were talking about events over the last few days, since they had last met. Nothing that was going to change the world, but the subject somehow moved on to time off work.

"We all need time away from work at some point," Eddie stated.

The others sat there somewhat amused. John looked at Eddie, with complete disbelief on his face, and then briefly glanced at Morris and Gary. He looked back at Eddie.

"And this "time away from work" needed is precisely how long in your opinion?" he quizzed after those few seconds of silent disbelief.

"Well it depends on the pressure of your job, I suppose. But the point I'm trying to make is that everyone needs a holiday."

"Life is one bloody great big holiday for you! And you wouldn't know what pressure was if it jumped up and bit you on the arse!" exclaimed John.

"Well, I'm only saying that a change of scenery is sometimes needed. Some, well most, go on holiday once or twice a year, others emigrate or travel. You know, that kind of thing."

Morris interjected, "It's also a way of meeting new people."

"Jesus, have they put something in your bloody beer," Gary said sarcastically. "I needed to prepare myself more for this evening, had I known that you two were going to get all philosophical."

Emigrating, travelling abroad had, of course, hit a little nerve with John, unbeknown to the others. If he was going to mention what was really on his mind, now was the time. Not because he wanted to make Eddie feel awkward, or get into a particularly heavy conversation (as heavy as it could be with these guys), but it did occur to him in these last few minutes, that actually a holiday wasn't a bad idea. He decided to go for it.

"Actually, that's what Jo's decided to do with her mum." There, said it. Now he needed to prepare himself for questions and comforting words of wisdom. Some would be bordering on useful, but it was likely that most would have the best intentions but be of no use at all.

"Do what?" asked Gary.

"Emigrate. Move abroad. However you wanna put it. To Spain"

"Shit!" exclaimed Gary

In truth, John had completely misjudged the reaction he would get. It stopped the conversation in an instant, and he actually began to regret saying anything. Even Morris and Eddie didn't really know what to say, but Eddie cemented his ability to be inappropriate.

"And Spanish men are not to be trusted!"

"Brilliant!" exclaimed Gary again. "Eddie, mate, you open your mouth and inappropriateness just comes pouring out!"

Morris, who had been strangely quiet up to this juncture, then showed a side of him that had never been seen before. A somewhat sympathetic nature.

"So, er…" He hesitated and sounded slightly uncomfortable. "When did you find out about this?"

"Last night. Jo dropped the bombshell as we sat at home. Turns out her mother has been planning this for five months, and not deemed it necessary to let me in on her secret plans she has for her and her daughter." He emphasised the words in his sentence, to stress the fact that it seemed to him, obvious in decisions like this, his feelings didn't appear to matter.

"Surely she can't do that without your permission, can she?" Morris asked, showing support. Which John welcomed, and it encouraged him to continue.

"Well, I guess she can if Jo wants to do it. I wouldn't want to be the bad guy. If she was trying to drag Jo kicking and screaming, then that would be different, but I think she quite likes the idea. I know she doesn't like the thought of being so far away from me, but she's old enough to make her own mind up."

There was a pause.

"Doesn't stop it pissing me off beyond belief, though," John concluded.

"Right, well I'll get the drinks in then," Eddie said, breaking the silence.

"Bugger me, something good has come out of it then," Joked Gary, trying to lift the atmosphere.

"Did he work today then?" John asked Morris.

"Yep, and he got some rebate back from the social, or somethin', so make the most of it."

John turned towards the bar. "Three packets of peanuts, and one for yourself," he said.

Not really sure if John wanted to say any more on the subject, Gary thought he'd ask another question and see what the response was.

"So, when's this all happening then? I mean, when are they going?"

"Seems it's all set for when Jo finishes college in July. I don't know how soon after. I don't know what she is planning in terms of her A levels. I don't know how long it's for. In fact, it stunned me so much last night, I didn't do a very good job in finding out the detail."

John paused for a moment, and then made his confession.

"In fact, I was so concerned about how hard done by I was, I didn't ask anything really. Which is a bit crap. Then to cap it all, this morning as I dropped Jo off at college, I came out with some bollocks about she wouldn't miss me coz she'd be having too good a time. So now my daughter's not even talking to me."

"You don't know that," Gary said. "She'll understand you were upset; she's a bright kid, she'll be okay."

They had all met Jo, as she had ventured down to the pub on a couple of evenings with her dad, when they met to watch footie and have a couple of beers. She liked them all, and they did make her laugh for various reasons, She was surprised, however, that her dad had the patience with Morris and Eddie.

Eddie returned from the bar. He placed the drinks on the table then and sat down. John stared at him.

"The peanuts will be where then?"

"Oh, I thought that was your little joke," replied Eddie and then continued: "So, back to my original comments." He paused and looked at everyone, but no one quite knew to which of his comments he referred. John was agitated by Eddie's complete dismissal of the peanut saga, but let it drop.

"Everyone needs some time away. You know, a holiday."

"Fuck me, Eddie," Gary quickly interjected

"No, no, I mean because of that, you know, Spain thing, we should all go away somewhere. You know, change of scenery; have a laugh, few beers, that sort of thing."

The other three were all independently thinking the same. A holiday would be fantastic, a holiday together, hadn't really considered that?

"And I have the perfect plan," continued Eddie.

Which immediately intrigued the others.

"To make it a great laugh, we go camping!" Eddie finished his statement, and waited to be congratulated on such a brilliant idea.

There was an initial silence. John, Gary and Morris were slightly taken aback by the thought. John's initial reaction was not exactly in favour. A holiday with these guys had some potential, but a holiday camping? Absolutely no chance whatsoever!

"Are you insane?" John's tone emphasised the strength of his feeling.

"Why camping?" asked Gary.

There was a slight pause,

"Camping, and in Wales!" Morris said proudly.

Gary and John looked at each other. It was no surprise to either of them that those two were on the same wavelength.

"Perfect," Eddie eagerly agreed. "Morris can tell us where best to go, and we just go and have a laugh." He paused, "And get pissed a bit."

"I ask again. Why camping? Why can't we just book into a B&B or somethin'?"

John joined forces. "Does anyone actually own any camping equipment? And why would we want to live like tramps for however long?"

"Because it would be a laugh, and booking into a hotel, or whatever, would be boring," Eddie argued.

"I think I could probably get us some tents," Morris added.

To Gary and John it almost seemed that Morris and Eddie already had this planned, and it certainly explained why the topic of conversation had made it round to "getting away".

"No, I just thought of it, and I think it's a brilliant idea," Eddie said.

"Well, lads," Morris said. "What about it?"

Neither John nor Gary could deny that some time away, having some beers, and having a laugh, was a good idea. They just weren't sure this was how they would do it. The discussion continued for a while, and whilst Morris was unable to give too much assurance regarding the obtaining of necessary camping equipment, John and Gary came round to the way of thinking that anything was probably worth trying.

They were 'happy' to let Morris advise on location, although Gary did make the point that after eighteen years away, Morris would be basing his decision on somewhat out-of-date information.

"Well, I know a really nice, small village called Dale, that won't have changed much. It's as south as you can go, has the sea either side of it and, more importantly, it has a pub, and there are plenty of fields to camp in. It's quite beautiful," Morris stated with certainty.

"Beautiful?" John paused. "If only we knew what your definition of beautiful was."

"Well you'll find out," replied Morris defensively. He remembered it was beautiful, 18 years ago, and back then, it did have a pub!!

It was agreed that Morris would sort the equipment and book the campsite, although that would come later as a date was still to be decided. John would need to find out exactly when Jo was leaving, and Gary had "a supplier's meeting" sometime in July.

"A supplier's meeting!" exclaimed John. That in itself sounded dodgy, given that Gary never gave any detail on who they were, where they came from, or indeed where the merchandise originated from. No one pursued it, though, as Gary's standard answer was always "it's all above board", which of course, it wasn't. Morris would have no problem booking the time off work, and Eddie was ready to go now.

The remainder of the evening was spent discussing the trip. Attempts were made to make a list of all their camping requirements; how they would get there; what tent or tents they should have; what implements they needed; but as the evening wore on, and more alcohol was consumed, it got silly, and actually became apparent that there was more to camping than they had initially thought. To Morris and Eddie it became a case of, "We'll sort that when we get there."

They left the pub and agreed to meet in a couple of weeks (various events prevented it being earlier), and they would see how far Morris and Eddie had progressed with the arrangements. John and Gary walked a short way together.

"This will be a disaster," John said. "You do realise? Letting those two make the arrangements." His tone was light-hearted and not one of concern.

"Yeah well, you know I thought that." Agreed Gary. "But then I thought sod it, I'm already risking disaster by agreeing to go, so the fact that there will be bugger all organised, and there's a good chance we will have no tents, and no campsite even contacted, let alone booked, is bizarrely part of the attraction."

John noted that Gary was being uncharacteristically thoughtful about it, but at the same time decided he was probably just showing John that he was with him or that too much alcohol was making him a bit philosophical.

"Yeah," John agreed and sighed. "Right now the thought of being able to lose myself in an abysmally arranged two-week camping debacle, is strangely attractive."

The two parted to go their separate ways. On the remainder of the walk, and until he finally drifted off to sleep, once in bed, John thought about how he would make sure he and Jo were back on good terms. He considered how to approach the Spain move with her mother, and that, he was actually rather looking forward to some time away with guys who had very few cares in the world. It might just be what he will need to look forward to, following that fateful day Jo leaves.

Morris returned home wondering if he had made one suggestion too many. He really wanted to go on a holiday like this, and the other guys were great company. That part would be a laugh. To suggest the location, however, was a bold one. Dale was a great little village, he remembered, but that wasn't all he needed to consider. But he had time to back out or change the location, so he tried to put it to the back of his mind, and concentrated on finishing his chips and curry sauce – the obligatory after pub indulgence.

CHAPTER THREE

"So, how's it goin' then?" Eddie asked, waiting to be told that everything had been arranged, and there was no need for him to do a single thing.

"Slow," Morris replied, drawing the word out, to emphasise very, very slow.

In fact, it had gone so "slow" that Morris hadn't actually done anything in the last week. He had met up with Eddie in the pub, despite the other two not being available, because "we can compare notes, and see what still remains to be done by the time we meet with the guys next week," Morris had suggested.

In reality, they both sat there with their drinks, and concluded there was still much to do….in fact, all of it still to do!

"I did ask Simon at work if he'd ever been camping." Morris began. "Wanted to know if he could give me some pointers as to what was needed, and where the best places were to shop for stuff we'd need. More importantly, how much it would all cost."

"So what did he recommend?" asked Eddie.

"He's never been camping," came the reply.

"Oh, bummer!" exclaimed Eddie. The conversation stopped.

This is where Morris and Eddie's plan had hit a slight snag. Two weeks away, on the piss, and it not costing very much was the plan, and for that they needed to be on holiday with John and Gary. For about thirty seconds, whilst they were in the pub together some weeks ago hatching this 'plan', they had an attack of conscience. It could seem to the outsider that they only wanted John and Gary there to pay for the holiday.

"I would have no problem saying that I love those two guys like they were my brothers," Morris had slurred in justification.

"Me, too," agreed Eddie.

So they continued, their evening, with clear consciences. It was nothing to do with the need for 'financial security', it was genuine friendship that was the driving force.

So, their plan had been successful up to a point. However, now they actually needed to do something, and this wasn't their forte.

"Right. Tomorrow is Saturday, and we go and buy a tent and a stove. Or at least order them," Morris said quite definitely, realising that he didn't want to be in a position where he was required to pay for the stuff.

Who was Eddie to argue; apart from his own clothes, he couldn't think of anything else they would need for camping. So that was all sorted, and the subject took no further part in their discussions that evening.

Neither Morris nor Eddie had much of an idea where to buy camping equipment. Army and Navy stores seemed to be a thing of the past, and Eddie couldn't recall ever having seen a shop name with 'camping' in it. Neither could look on the internet, because that was beyond both of them. Besides which, neither of them possessed a computer. So, in the middle of town they were, and as to where they should be heading... they had no clue.

Morris decided to stop and ask the most attractive woman he could find to ask if she knew where there was a camping shop. She was attractive, so he didn't really care whether she knew of one or not.

"Excuse me," he almost pleaded, and she stopped to look at him. The next bit he didn't really bargain for. He felt at that very moment as if he were going to sneeze. He tried to wiggle his nose, to make it go away, so immediately the girl thought he had an affliction. She stared at him and moved her head back slightly. Before he could ask the question, the sneeze arrived. He tried to stifle it as best he could, but this resulted in asserting tremendous pressure in his nose. The sneeze was controlled. What wasn't controlled was the amount of matter it forced out of his nose, on to his top lip and surrounding area. He knew something had happened, because he had put his hand up to cover his mouth and nose, so some of it was now forming a bridge across to his hand. In the absence of a tissue, Morris turned away as soon as he could, not realising that Eddie was directly behind him, so his hand and some of its contents rubbed randomly on to Eddie's shirt. It took Eddie a couple of seconds to realise he had taken a share of the deposits, because as Morris turned, Eddie didn't initially understand what had happened. His immediate reaction was to push Morris off, and as he did, something sort of long and transparent seemed to be connected to them both, then break its connection with Morris's hand, and slap on to Eddie's shirt.

The lady was heard to say "Bless you", but only faintly because she had continued on her journey to wherever she was headed, which didn't involve being stopped by men just in time to see them blow snot over themselves.

"Oh for fuck sake, what the…?" Eddie was going to ask what it was, but he knew very well that the front of his shirt now had a moist, snotty patch about five centimetres long, just left of centre, below the collar.

"You dirty bastard, look at this."

Morris didn't reply. He was trying desperately to remove any trace of the offending matter from his face, using the only thing he had, which was the back of his hand. To make matters worse, he then sneezed again, which whilst it didn't contain the same density of matter, still provided more substance to deal with.

So Morris and Eddie spent the next five minutes looking for the public toilets, so that Morris could wipe all the snot off his hands and anywhere else it was, and Eddie could lift the offending small but very visible moist amount from off his shirt.

Whilst they were looking, they both began to see the funny side.

"She was really impressed, I could tell," Eddie joked

"You don't think any landed on her, do you?" Morris asked, and this thought amused him, so he pursued it.

"I mean, she could now be walking around town, thinking she looks okay, but with a little dangly bit hanging from her hair. Imagine that, when she next looks in a mirror!"

"At some point, she will run her fingers through her hair." Eddie motioned the act, and the resulting study of the hand, followed by the imaginary heaving.

Cleaned up, although the wet patch on Eddie's shirt drew attention to the fact that he had obviously tried to remove something unwanted from it, they re-joined the bustle of the town centre. They decided that Argos was the best bet, but they weren't exactly sure of the most direct route to the store. A few side street 'short cuts' later, and they were not feeling confident of being any closer to the store

"Where are we?" Eddie asked.

"Reading," came the evasive answer from Morris.

As they turned the corner, walking into a side street which they thought they recognised, Morris saw a shop sign which looked promising. As they approached it, they could see the window clearly stating:

'GO CAMPING IN STYLE'

"Right, perfect. We get some prices of tents and stoves, then we're out of here. It's thirsty work this, and I need a drink," Morris stated defiantly, as he entered the shop. Eddie, in silent agreement, followed.

Obviously a camping specialist store, it was quickly evident to the both of them that camping was more than just a tent and stove. This place had everything so it seemed. A fairly big shop, it had tents of all shapes and sizes erected, all set up in little camping 'scenes'. This is where they started to realise that perhaps they had under-cooked the 'camping requirements' part.

"Fuck yeah, sleeping bags." Eddie said.

"Yeah." Morris was almost in deep thought. "Gas for the stove, a torch, kettle, pans, mugs…"

"And pillows," Eddie joined in, as they wandered aimlessly round. "Survival kit, look!" he exclaimed.

"Where the fuck do you think we're going?" Morris reacted. "The jungle?!"

"Well, Wales might not be as dangerous, but needing to survive flooding might come into it."

Morris ignored the rather obvious reply. His eye was taken with a tent, quite obviously meant for at least four people, and he decided it was worth a look inside.

"This would be perfect," he said as he paused momentarily, before entering. Eddie, who had been checking out seats, looked over, and hastily made his way to where Morris was. It seemed Morris had found luxury five star tent accommodation. It was set in its own little camping scene, with synthetic grass flooring, chairs and stove also outside, and the blue and grey tent looking very resplendent, conjuring up the perfect camping scene, which of course it was supposed to.

Morris had entered by the time Eddie arrived on the scene, so wanting to also check out the interior, Eddie didn't stop outside, he moved straight in. As he was in such a rush, he didn't notice that the very edge of the synthetic grass was slightly turned upwards.

As his foot caught the edge, the grass flooring followed him, and dismantled the neat arrangement of stove, table, and chairs. These in turn, crashed into the display of pots and pans. The noise this created was enough to turn the shop from a very peaceful business-like atmosphere, into one of commotion. Eddie tripped with enough forward momentum that he was sent uncontrollably into the frontage of the tent. He missed the entrance, and as he hit the front wall of the tent, his weight forced the guy ropes away from their secured positions, giving some of the pots and pans extra impetus as they crashed towards the tent.

The poles supporting the main structure of the tent, also gave way. Eddie, and the entire display, all landed on Morris with a force that knocked him to the floor. He was buried, completely out of sight, under all of it.

In the space of five seconds, Eddie had raised the mock camp site, to the ground.

There was a moment of silence, as members of staff tried to comprehend what had just occurred. Morris was trying to find a way out of the tent, which had completely engulfed him. Eddie was still on top of him and he was beginning to panic.

"Get the fuck off!" came the muffled shout from the floor.

Eddie quickly scrambled to his feet, and started tugging at the tent to free Morris. When he managed to clear it so that Morris was visible, he immediately apologised, but his tone of voice was more in humour than in sincerity.

"Sorry, mate," he said. "Don't know what happened there." He reached to give Morris a help up. "But I tell you what, it's a good job we tested this one, coz it's not very robust."

By now, the three members of staff, who until this point had made a very good job of ignoring Morris and Eddie, stood transfixed, as they pervade the disaster area. A display they were once proud of, had been reduced to a pile of product and bodies. Their response to the scene of devastation was a cross between amusement, and concern that the customers were okay.

"Are you okay, sir?" the young female assistant asked, making her way towards Morris.

"Yes. I'm fine, thanks," he quickly replied before kicking a saucepan out the way, and looking at Eddie. He was about to say something along the lines of "What the fuck happened", when he noticed that Eddie was watching the more senior member of staff, who was standing there, red faced, writing something down on a pad of paper.

Morris had now recovered from the shock of one moment standing inside a tent, the next having it collapse in on him, with a fifteen stone weight behind it, and a host of pots and pans crashing all around him, and was now seeing the funny side of it. Once he had regained his composure, Eddie just found the whole thing very amusing.

Both smiling, if just a little embarrassed, they made their way towards the senior assistant, who had his back to them.

"Sorry about that," Eddie said in a way which vaguely sounded sincere. But as he said it, he was not interested in a response, he was trying to peer over the senior assistant's shoulder, to find out what he was writing. The other two members of staff made a move to start clearing up, and the senior assistant, clearly not impressed with having the shop rearranged, turned to Eddie.

"Would you gentlemen require some assistance?"

Asked in such an aloof manner, only served to wind Morris up.

"Shame we had to go through all this to attract your attention," he said sarcastically.

The senior assistant shuffled uncomfortably, thought about a reply, and then thought better of it. Faced with a choice of helping to clear the mess up, or dealing with the two people who had destroyed his peaceful morning, he decided to continue, feeling confident he could ensure their fairly rapid departure.

"I assume from this," he gestured towards the mess on the floor, "that you would be interested in purchasing camping equipment?"

"Brilliant!" Morris exclaimed, at a volume the rest of the staff could hear too.

The senior assistant was not the only one who could show attitude. And now that he had put him in his place, he asked, "How much is that tent?" pointing to the one he and Eddie had just demolished.

"Six hundred and ninety-five pounds, sir," came the reply, in that *you can't afford that can you* tone.

Eddie turned his head away, and Morris who clearly didn't have any intention of losing this battle, hesitated momentarily before replying. "Is that the best price you can do?"

The assistant guessed that his assumption was right, and decided to put Morris down a little more.

"Well, sir. This one"—pointing to the one they had destroyed—"is now a little, shall we say, shop soiled. So I could let you have it for six-fifty?!"

Morris saw his get out. "So, you have dangerous flooring, which my friend trips over, sends us both crashing into items which, quite frankly, could have caused serious injury. I choose not to take that line, hope that we can still do business, and you take the piss by giving me forty-five quid off? You're a joke, mate." He gestured to Eddie, "Come on, this idiot obviously doesn't want our business, so let's get out of here."

With that, they both made a hasty exit, not giving the assistant any chance to react.

Once outside, and a few yards away from the shop, they were able to let their true reactions out.

"Seven hundred quid! Fuck me!" exclaimed Eddie, laughing.

"No, I did get him down to six-fifty," Morris reminded him.

"I think you'll find it was me that instigated the reduction," Eddie said. "And what was that about 'dangerous flooring'? You were in the tent, and then buried under it, so saw nothin'."

"Well, I wasn't goin' to let that little jumped up twat get one over on me. He knew we weren't in the market for somethin' that expensive, so we needed to get out of there quick."

They continued walking but relived the "tent crash" as they went. They also decided that maybe Argos was the place to head for. It was probably going to be more in their price bracket.

Half an hour later, they were on their way home, catalogue in hand, feeling that they deserved a beer for their troubles. They had now put together a list of items they needed to buy, and would talk the other two through it, the following week in the pub.

That following week, in the pub, it wasn't as plain sailing as Morris and Eddie thought it would be.

"So in all, it will cost us a hundred and twenty quid, and we'll have everything we need," Morris concluded.

"That's four tents, sleeping bags, pans, stove, everything?" John said, just wanting to clarify, because Morris hadn't brought the catalogue to the pub as he didn't want to carry it.

"Er, not four tents. Two," corrected Morris slightly hesitant because he knew what was coming. "That way we save money," he added, "and one to take all four of us, is more expensive too."

John and Gary had to admit that sharing a tent, whilst who shared with who had not yet been discussed, would be more in keeping with the whole experience. There was some hesitancy about letting Morris and Eddie buy all of the equipment, but nevertheless, John and Gary agreed to give them their share of the cost next time they met up.

"Well," Morris and Eddie said almost simultaneously. Morris continued: "Thing is, we're a bit short at the moment, and…"

"You want us to pay for it," interrupted John. "Okay, I'll pay for the equipment, just make sure you don't cock it up."

John was actually quite surprised it was only going to cost that much, and he was earning a good living, so it wasn't really a problem to pay it. Nobody tried to talk him out of it, including Gary, so John agreed to let Morris have the money. Morris was also going to sort out a campsite, and John wondered how long it would be before he was asked to fund the deposit. They also decided that the first two weeks of August would be good to go. Jo had told John that July 31st was the date they were leaving, so August 1st was perfect timing for him. Gary's supplier's meeting would also have happened by then.

All seemed settled. Morris and Eddie achieved their goal of a funded holiday. Gary was happy going "on the piss" for two weeks, and the thought of a holiday romance had also entered his head. John didn't want the time to arrive, but knew he would need something to help him through the first couple of weeks, so this bizarre event was perfect timing. He still needed to have conversations, which he also wasn't looking forward to.

CHAPTER FOUR

"Well these things happen, John, and we can't leave until the third," Susan, his ex-wife rather patronisingly explained.

Their move to Spain had been delayed a few days. This now resulted in John actually going on the camping trip before Jo left, because he and his "band of merry men" as Jo now referred to them as, were leaving on the 1st. This hadn't pleased him because he had wanted to be there until she finally left.

John and Susan had met some weeks before, and John expressed his frustration at Susan not mentioning this to him, when she had made her first serious enquires. Susan had apologised, John wasn't convinced she really meant it, but there was little point in trying to challenge it either from an emotional angle or indeed a legal one. He was sure that Jo wanted to do this, and he knew she wished he would be there too; so as much as it was tearing him up, he had to accept it was how it was going to be. He would take every opportunity he could to visit, or fly Jo over to the UK. This thought didn't make it all okay, but it did ease the stress a little.

During the eight or nine weeks since receiving the news from Jo, John had spent more time with his daughter, which he was happy about, engrossed himself in work, which had brought its rewards, and in a slightly apprehensive way, also looked forward to his holiday. He had been determined not to feel sorry for himself, and make sure he and Jo parted on good terms. They ate out, went to the cinema, on sunny days they had visited the coast, and for a week they took a trip to the Canaries for some relaxing time together. In fact, up to two days before he left for Wales, John felt their time together had been just perfect. He wasn't sure it would make the parting any easier, but he was in a good place with their relationship, and that was the most important factor to him. The last two days, however, were to undo some of this, and their parting would not go to plan.

Armed with the cash, which John had given them, Morris and Eddie had bought what they considered to be, 'the essentials' for the trip.

"Tents, sleeping bags, stove, pots, kettle. Sorted," Morris stated with authority to Eddie.

On the next time they all met up, Morris proudly announced to John and Gary that he and Eddie had everything needed for the trip.

"Two tents, four sleeping bags, a stove, some pots, a kettle. I think we're all set," he announced.

There was a brief silence.

"And do the tents come with all rope things needed to tie them down, and groundsheets?" John asked.

"Er, yep," Morris answered with an air of uncertainty.

"Maybe you better check, just to be sure," John suggested as he knew perfectly well that this hadn't even entered their heads.

"Gas, for the stove?" John added.

"Good point." Replied Morris

"Something to drink out of, eat on, and with?" John was now beginning to realise "all set" perhaps wasn't quite true.

"Nice one." Morris sounded a little hesitant, as he also began to realise there was probably more.

"And the campsite is booked, presumably?" John continued his questioning.

"Yeah, yeah, in hand." Morris was now sounding slightly agitated. The other three knew his answer meant "No".

"So does this mean you need more money?" John asked, knowing the answer.

"Well, I don't think I need much. Got a little bit left over." Answered Morris.

"And I'm drinking it, I suppose?" John said, assuming that was why Morris bought the first round.

The subject moved on to other incidentals, like how they were travelling there and back. As only Gary and John owned a car, and Gary's seemed to need a service every fifty miles, John volunteered to drive, in order to save time on the discussion. They would set out early on the Friday morning. They got bogged down on whether they should all get to John's, or he should pick them up. A discussion that went on far too long in his opinion, and ended with him agreeing to picking them all up en route.

"And when we get there, I'll make sure both tents are put up, the stove is on, and make you all a cup of tea. Anything else I can do to make your stay comfortable, let me know," John concluded, sarcastically.

After a moment's pause, "Brilliant. A telly would be good," Eddie joked.

John looked at him. "I'll see what I can do, sir." Eddie chose to say nothing further.

Only two days to go, and John's mind wasn't really on the holiday. He had planned with Jo and Susan to fly out to Spain at the beginning of September, so he hadn't got too long to wait, but the thought that she wasn't going to be in the same country as him on a daily basis, was his biggest hurdle. However, this was how it was going to be, so he had to face up to it.

Nearing the actual date was obviously playing on Jo's mind too. She was a little subdued, and whilst the two of them were together, the atmosphere felt awkward to both, knowing what was about to happen, and neither knowing how to deal with it. John was a little short on patience and his temperament edgy. Jo was trying to please her father, so it was an uneasy last two days they were due to be together. As far as John understood, Jo was staying with him Thursday night, and he was dropping her back to her mother's on the morning he was leaving. Then came the finale to all the stress and frustration.

"Mum has arranged for us to have dinner with her friends tomorrow night," Jo informed him on Wednesday.

"Why my last night with you?" he exclaimed, so frustrated it was all he could do not to let out a barrage of expletives. "She could have arranged that for over the weekend, once I have gone."

"I don't know, you will have to speak to mum."

"How old are you?" he asked sarcastically. "Are you not old enough to say, 'Mum it's my last night with dad, and I'd prefer it if you arranged it for another night,'" he protested. "Or does that not matter, and you're doing what you want to do anyway?"

Jo knew this was not going to please her dad, but she didn't reckon on being accused of wanting to part with him, so she could get on with her 'new more exciting life', which was the accusation in his voice. So any reply she gave, wasn't going to be good enough.

"People couldn't make it over the weekend, so she said it was going to have to be the Thursday."

"Well, don't mind me," he paused. "I wouldn't want to spoil the party." John was angry, upset, and didn't really know what to do or say. So he just did his usual, and slammed a few doors on his way round the house. He wasn't going anywhere in particular, he just wanted to walk through a few doors so he could slam them. This was his language for "I'm angry", which Jo clearly understood.

So the rest of the evening was practically silent, apart from the occasional slammed door, and then once Jo had gone to bed, he called Susan.

"John, it's half past eleven!" Susan exclaimed.

"I don't give a shit!" he yelled back, hoping Jo hadn't heard him. "Jo tells me you have arranged a dinner for tomorrow night, so I just wanted to thank you for not only taking my daughter away from me, but fuckin' up my last night with her, too."

"Well, I'm sorry it worked out that way, but I didn't know you were going away when I arranged it." Susan's defence was logical, but that just annoyed him more. He was beyond being reasonable. He was the one losing out here, and he had every right to feel sorry for himself.

"Oh that's right," he began sarcastically. "It's my fault. Might have bloody known," and he hung up. No point prolonging the conversation. Susan was going to stick by her claim. It was right, but he was angry and having very little in the way of a comeback made him a bit speechless. He didn't want Susan to know that, so putting the phone down on her made sure she didn't get the upper hand.

He didn't sleep much that night, as he was emotionally charged. By morning, he wasn't really in any better mood. Today was the last day, so he felt upset by that, and neither Jo nor her mum had apologised. Yes, Susan had said she was sorry it worked out like that, but that didn't mean she was really sorry, it was just a figure of speech. However, if he thought none of this could get any worse, he was wrong.

He showered and dressed, ready to spend their last day like a last day should be spent. He was going to have to put all his frustration and emotion to one side, and make sure they had a good last day. However, he wasn't ready for what 'hit' him when he entered the lounge.

Jo was already sat there, dressed and bag packed.

"I need to go back to mum's now because I have loads of stuff to do," she said in a slightly nervous low voice.

John was stunned. He didn't really know what to say. This was no way to part, but something inside of him stopped him from pleading with her to stay a while. She had obviously decided it was best to part now. Hopefully, by the time they met up in September, things would have been forgotten, and their happiness at seeing each other again would erase these heated exchanges. This was John's quick summary of the situation, and not wanting to cause a continuation of hostilities, he said, "Okay, well, make sure you have everything, and I'll grab my keys." There was obvious sadness, and disappointment in his voice.

They had difficulty looking at each other, and there was certainly no conversation once they were in the car. John was desperate to break the silence. Jo sat there, looking straight ahead, but thinking exactly the same thing. The journey, however, dictated that time was up, and both of them had failed miserably to at least patch things up. They were now outside Susan's house, and John needed this bit over as quickly as possible. As tears welled up, he turned to Jo.

"Have a safe journey, and I'll call you soon."

"Dad," Jo replied, also feeling the emotion grabbing hold. "Whatever you may think, this is as hard for me. You seem to think I have this new, exciting life ahead, and that I've already written you out of it. It's not fair that you accuse me of not considering you, when actually all you are doing is thinking how hard this is for you." As the emotion took hold, her voice became louder, but quivered. Tears overflowed, and Jo attempted to wipe them away as she continued.

"There's a part of my life I don't like, and if I could change it I would. I hate not seeing you every day. When I'm with you, I hate not seeing mum every day. But I have no choice, and I get on with it. You two force me to make these decisions, and they are decisions I wish I never had to make. But when I do, I don't expect my parents to tell me I'm only doing what I want."

She stopped, and frantically searched for a tissue in her bag. Not being able to find one, and John wasn't even looking her way. He had turned to look out his window, with tears rolling down his face, Jo continued with her outburst.

"Maybe what I'm doing is for the best, then when I'm doing what 'I want to do', it doesn't affect you. I love you, dad, but now I have to go."

With that, she opened the car door, grabbed her bags, and left, closing the door behind her, giving John no chance to say anything. Within seconds she had disappeared into the house.

John sat there for a few minutes. He was lost somewhere in a world that he had only ever visited once before—the day he left Jo with her mum. Emotionally shattered, and having been put firmly in his place, he was completely motionless. Eventually, he realised he was still sitting outside Susan's house, so he quickly put the car into gear, and drove away. The car that was approaching from behind as he did so, was not too impressed, but did find out that brakes and ABS were working perfectly.

Once he thought he had the better of his emotions, anger started to creep in. He blamed Jo. He blamed Susan. In fact, he blamed the world. This was not supposed to happen, and he refused to accept that he should take the blame for a situation he had no control over. He could be 'hard-nosed' too, so he had a holiday with the lads to look forward to. He was going to enjoy it, probably get pissed a number of times, and have a bloody good laugh. That's what the doctor would order him to do.

CHAPTER FIVE

For some reason John knew that pick up this morning was not going to run smoothly. When Morris and Eddie were involved, things rarely did go according to plan. Gary was first, and indeed ready, when John arrived. Only a small suitcase, and a pillow, so timing and space for luggage, still on track. On the way to Morris's, where they were to pick up both Morris and Eddie, John inquired how the previous evening had gone, as the three of them had met for "a quick couple of beers", after the 'intense' packing. John hadn't gone because he wanted to be at home when Jo called. Jo didn't call, and when John had tried to call her, her mobile was off. A result of them being at "the last supper", as John mumbled to himself.

"When I left them, they were on their fourth of two pints, and both were discussing the finer points of the art of camping. As they are now both experts of course," Gary said sarcastically.

"And you left at what time?" John asked.

"'Bout ten."

"Oh bollocks. That means they would have been pissed when they left by eleven. It's now seven thirty, and there's what chance of them being up, never mind actually being ready?" John said.

Gary was on his mobile trying Morris's number. "Voicemail," he said, turning his head towards John with the phone still to his ear. He paused, waited for the beep, "Morris, we're on our way. We'll be there in about ten minutes, so get the fuck up," he ordered, and ended the call.

They pulled up outside the small block of flats where Morris lived. No sign of life, just one of the older flat residents waiting for his dog to finish its early morning 'movement' on the front lawn, without a thought of producing a bag and disposing of it. John always maintained

33

he would never have a dog, "Why would I want to pick up dog shit?" was his reason. It also reminded him of the several requests for a dog, from Jo over the years. He always said "No" to her, because he would be the one who ended up walking it daily, once the novelty wore off. Picking up after it, he also mentioned on one occasion.

John realised that he was already thinking about Jo, and reminded himself that the previous evening he had concluded his trip in September would clear the air. That would allow him to concentrate on his holiday with the lads, not dwell on the crap situation with Jo. But he had to stop feeling cut up about their parting yesterday, and here he was, some twenty-four hours later, already finding it difficult to keep it locked away in the back of his mind.

Once out of the car, the two of them made their way to the front doors of Morris's block. There were only two blocks, and although the apartments were nothing fancy, and relatively cheap to rent, they seemed in good order, for properties built in the seventies.

"You can smell that dog shit from here," Gary said, obviously having made the same observation as John moments earlier. "Bastards should be made to eat the stuff they don't pick up. Wouldn't fuckin' do it again," he added.

They walked up to the first floor. There were only two flats on each level. Flat number three, Gary rang the doorbell.

"Why you doing that?" asked John anxiously, from a few feet away.

Gary looked round at him. "Bollocks, it's number four isn't it?" Gary whispered, creeping his way towards John, as if being quiet now would mean nobody inside number three heard the doorbell at seven-thirty in the morning.

John gently knocked on Morris's door. The door opened with a sharp pull, almost before John had finished knocking.

"We're up. We were up. Whatever!" Morris exclaimed loudly, trying to convince John and Gary that that was indeed the case.

"Just let us in a minute," Gary said.

Morris was slightly taken aback by their preoccupation of gaining entry into the flat, rather than his expected bollocking for not being ready.

"What's up?" he enquired.

"I just rang number three by mistake," Gary whispered.

Morris looked thoughtful for a second. "Dead," he stated after a moment's silence, turned and then moved towards the lounge, stepping over the various packed bags and heaps of camping equipment. Gary and John looked at each other.

"Dead? Who's dead?" Gary asked, as they followed him.

"Frank from number three. Died last week, in his sleep. Well, possibly the week before, coz nobody had seen him for days."

Neither Gary nor John were now really listening. They were more interested in the thrown back covers on the sofa, and the apparent absence of Eddie. Plus the evidence of late night pizza which lay strewn across the coffee table and floor. An ashtray full of roll up ends, also explained the stuffy smell, and all in all they were not getting a feeling that Morris was speaking the absolute truth when he claimed they "were up" when Gary called. It was a small flat. One bedroom, a lounge, a kitchen, and a bathroom, so Eddie couldn't be far.

"Just in the bathroom," Morris replied when John asked about Eddie's whereabouts.

"But everything is ready," he added

"Except you two aren't," Gary surmised.

Morris considered his answer before he gave it. "Yes, I think we're just about there," he concluded, looking around in uncertainty.

"Then you'll just be wanting to put your trousers on, and we'll be off," John said, as he turned towards the lounge door. "We may as well start putting this stuff in the car," he beckoned to Gary.

John knew that they should have a check list, but he also knew that Morris wouldn't have one, and he couldn't be bothered to start one now. He checked the important things, like tents, ground sheets, and sleeping bags. The rest they could check when they unloaded at the other end. As long as he had the capability to sleep and stay reasonably dry should it rain, the rest was secondary.

He and Gary managed to pile everything in to the car, with a bit of a struggle, and then made their way back upstairs for what they hoped was the final time. They hadn't been aware of anyone else about, but as they reached the first floor, they were just in time to see someone disappear into number three. They glanced at each other as this was a little surprising, given Morris's 'sensitive' update on the current residency situation there.

"Did Frank have a wife?" John asked, as they entered Morris's flat.

"Er, no. Don't think so, or else he would've bin found sooner I'm guessing," Morris answered confidently.

"Then how come we've just seen someone go in there?" John questioned.

As he said that, Eddie appeared behind them, as if he had just come through the front door. John turned, "Where…?" he started.

"Well," Morris said. "I figured that with Frank gone, he wouldn't have minded if I borrowed the flat when someone came to stay. Frank let me have a spare key for emergencies, so I'm sure he'd be okay about it."

"That way, I got to sleep in a bed too," Eddie said.

With slight hesitation, but knowing the answer before he asked it, John inquired, "Frank died in his sleep?" he said with a contorted expression. "And by in his sleep, I guess you mean in his bed… and you just spent the night in that bed?"

"No!" Gary exclaimed in a long, drawn out fashion.

"It was fine. I turned the pillow over." Eddie seemed quite at ease with it.

"That's fuckin' disgraceful." John put his hand to his mouth as he said it, to imitate throwing up. "I thought you slept here," he added, pointing at the obvious evidence of someone having slept on the sofa.

"No, that was me," Morris informed him. "I do that from time to time when I can't be bothered to move to the bedroom."

John just shook his head slightly, and neither he nor Gary could quite come to terms with Eddie having slept in a dead man's bed.

They loaded the last few things into the car, and were finally on their way. Only for about half a mile, however, because newspapers, tobacco, and a few cans "for later" were needed. Only a short time after that, John felt somewhat 'alone', as the other three made themselves comfortable and eventually dozed off, one by one.

John didn't mind, though. He found the monotony of the motorway ample time to make sure his mind was in the right place for these next two weeks. Jo would be gone, and although they hadn't parted on best terms, he would make that his priority once he was back, and his visit in September would be a happy one that he was already looking forward to. For now, he must put the sadness to one side, and enjoy the boys' company for two weeks. As he thought about it, he looked at them, Gary in the passenger seat, Morris and Eddie, through the rear view mirror, mouths open, heads flopping with no control. He smiled, and knew then that this was what he needed. A break from reality.

The 230 mile journey was only broken with one further stop, for cups of tea, food, and a visit to the loo. It turned out to be quite a lengthy stop as they were not in a hurry, and a mid-afternoon arrival would leave them enough time to erect the tents. None of them confessed to being experts at this, but Morris was confident in his own knowledge, gained whilst purchasing the equipment.

"How difficult can it be anyway?" Gary's comment almost dismissing the task as insignificant.

"Where exactly is the campsite?" John asked Morris whilst they were stopped.

The hesitation and glance at Eddie, gave him his answer immediately.

"Well…" Morris started.

"You haven't booked one, have you?" John said.

"Not exactly, no."

"What does that mean?" John asked.

"Er, no."

This was neither a surprise nor a problem to John as he knew aspects of this holiday would be 'ad hoc', or 'improvised'. It was part of the attraction; the break from reality. He smiled, "Fuck it, we'll find something when we get there."

"It's only a tiny place anyway," Morris said. "Pitchin' a couple of tents won't be a problem."

They all accepted his 'better knowledge', and the subject wasn't raised again until they arrived at the quaint seaside village of Dale, South Wales.

Morris was certainly right about one thing, Dale was small. In fact, one road led into it, up one side for about 700 metres, and then came round the other side about the same distance, with open field space in between. As they entered the village, they passed a pub, a small church, church hall, and a store serving also as a Post Office. Added to that was the relatively small number of residential houses and on their left was the sea, with a small harbour housing a number of small boats, fishing and leisure, a Marine store and a yacht club.

To check the place out, John drove round the village in its entirety. It took about five minutes. One fact they all agreed on, however, was that this was a beautiful part of the country, and probably not enough people got to see it. The last main town they had passed was Milford Haven, about ten miles to the east. They had also passed signs for Haverfordwest, which was to the north of Dale some thirteen miles away. So, they were also certainly away from "the rest of the world" as Gary effectively described it. The first building they obviously checked out was the pub, 'Griffin Inn'. An old building, but maintained in keeping with its age, they all instantly took a liking to it.

"Right, now we're here, might as well sample the local nectar." Eddie was eager to commence the holiday in the manner that he believed was its main purpose. Gary agreed, and Morris seemed okay with the suggestion, but he was not in as loud support as would have been expected. He was somewhat distracted by their surroundings, and appeared to be 'taking in' the scenery with more care than the others would give him credit for.

Eddie gave him a little nudge, "Pub?"

"Er, yeah, sounds good to me," Morris replied reluctantly.

"Hate to be a kill-joy," John interrupted. "But I reckon we should find somewhere to pitch, so that we know where we'll sleep tonight, and I can leave the car and not touch it again for two weeks. Then you can get as pissed as you like."

There was general agreement.

"Good point," Eddie said. "It shouldn't take long, and I'm sure we can find somewhere pretty close."

They drove once more, through the village towards the west. The sea was not far away in this direction either. Dale being situated almost as far south as you could get, so the sea surrounded it. As they came to Dale's most westerly point, John noticed a narrow, single track road heading off up the hill which he guessed might lead to some great views over the sea, and possibly an ideal campsite location.

"Let's have a look up here," John suggested. But as he had already turned into the road, the others didn't have a chance to voice any opinion. Except Eddie.

"Jesus, how far's this gonna be from the bloody pub?" he said, with more than a hint of alarm.

"There might not be anything up here," John said. "I know as much as you." The road was a very steep gradient.

"There are some fields up here," Morris said. Then added, "I remember coming up here years ago."

As they reached the top, the road levelled out and there was no sign of any campsite. Morris had been correct; the first piece of land on their right was a huge field separated from the road by a five foot wall constructed of stone. Although the road had levelled out, the field continued to climb, and they were obviously not quite at the top. The field seemed to disappear over the top of the hill, about a hundred or so metres away.

"Stop here a minute," Morris suggested. "Why don't we pitch here? There's nothing growing other than grass. This corner is out of sight from whatever's over the hill, and if we pitch fairly close to this stone wall, we'll be out of sight from the road. Free campin'!"

"Brilliant!" agreed Eddie. "Except it's too fuckin' far from the pub, and that hill will kill us all within days!"

John had pulled up at the gateway to the field, and they all got out. Each one of them knew this was not where tents were meant to be pitched, but the temptation was too much for them to resist.

"What's the worst that can happen? Someone comes and tells us to move," John said, knowing there was a high probability they would have to move at some point. Actually, they could get done for trespassing, or it could all just get taken away. "And if I park the car by the tents, close up against the wall, no one will ever know it's there." He wasn't totally convinced by that statement either, as it might get towed away, but he was past caring. He wanted no more responsibilities, no more decisions to make, just two weeks of bumming around and taking things as they happened, and they would happen, a little sooner than he anticipated.

Four grown men, erecting two basic 'two-man' tents was a sight to behold. Morris had insisted all along that he could 'lead' this part of the trip. *After all, how difficult can it be*, he had thought to himself, and had sounded this out on Eddie, who agreed he was the "man for the job". Morris took this as a vote of confidence, even though it was Eddie taking the opportunity to let someone else do it. Consequently, Eddie's participation was off-loading the car, rather than anything constructive. Morris also raised the subject of who shared a tent with who. John had assumed Morris and Eddie would be sharing.

"I thought you'd both want to share dead man's bed stories. Yu' know, 'the best dead man's bed I've ever slept in'," he said. The morning's revelation about Eddie's chosen sleeping arrangements still at the forefront of his mind.

Morris had chosen to ignore the comment because he had a motive to lead this discussion too. He always had a good laugh with Eddie, but his tendency to talk incessantly when drunk, even caused Morris to suggest he slept in the 'spare' flat the previous night, because Eddie was in full flow, and on an equal level with the verbal diarrhoea, was the fact that the subject matter, as usual, swayed between women, sex, politics and drinking. Of these subjects, Eddie only experienced drinking on a regular basis, and once he got to the subject of standing at the next election for his own independent party, Morris knew it was time. Reckoning that his best chance of at least some sleep would be to share with John, he quickly suggested it, positioning himself in front of John and Gary.

"Eddie and I know each other, and this holiday gives us a chance to bond with you two guys, so John I'll share with you." He looked at Gary, "And you guys take the other."

He really hoped there would be no objections. Gary just shrugged his shoulders. He didn't really care. This was a lads' holiday, and hours of uninterrupted sleep wasn't very high on his expected list, so who he shared the tent with was irrelevant. John wasn't too concerned, either. He was probably getting the better deal of the two. If Eddie could sleep in a dead man's bed, what other frightening habits did he have? He would rather find out from somebody else having to endure them.

From the moment they realised Morris had forgotten to buy a relatively vital piece of equipment—a mallet—it was evident the process was going to take significantly longer than it should. Morris was unanimously sent into the village to rectify his mistake. He returned almost an hour later, which seemed an extraordinarily long time. When questioned, Morris claimed it was necessary to ask in the pub, as to where he could buy such an implement. The reason for the time taken, was immediately clear.

Arguments ensued over the position of the two tents, relative to each other. Many challenges arose. Was it possible to put up a tent inside out? Working out why the ropes were slack on one side and when tightened they pulled the pegs out the other side. The flysheet always touched the inner somewhere, threatening the tents waterproof capabilities. These were just a few of the issues. Morris quickly realised he wasn't quite the 'expert' he thought he was, and halfway through, the rain came. It became increasingly likely that for the first couple of nights at least, sleeping outside the tents was probably going to be more comfortable and dryer. At one point, they were beginning to think that Morris had successfully bought tents which contained the wrong sized poles, such was the tightness of the fit. They had also started by erecting the inner parts of the tent first, which proved to be the wrong method when it began raining. But no one had even given that a thought, so consequently once they had rushed to put the fly sheets up, it had indeed stopped raining. The flysheets were perfectly dry, and the inner sheets were wet.

It was almost 5pm before they were in a position to trust that the tents were going to stay up, and remain sturdy enough to actually start putting their personal belongings in.

"We'll designate that area over by the wall, just past the car, as the pisser," Morris indicated with a half gesture of his hand. In fact, the only reason he suggested it was because his swift pint whilst purchasing a mallet, had made its way through his system. As he stood against the wall, he turned his head back towards the others,

"And if you want a shit, bury it!" He turned his head back to concentrate on his aim.

"If you want a shit, wait 'til you get to the pub, you dirty bastard," John insisted.

"What about, you know, washin' and stuff like that?" Gary asked. "I'm not going out at night smellin' like a tramp."

Truth be known, none of them had thought this through.

"Well, we can buy water to wash in, and we'll have to check out what's in the village," John suggested.

Morris returned to the tents. "I'll check out the yacht club; might be showers and stuff there."

"Yeah, right," John replied with more than a hint of scepticism in his voice. "They're gonna welcome us with open arms."

He then mimicked their response.

"Come in, chaps. Help yourself to the facilities. Our members pay hundreds to use the club; you're welcome to come and use them for fuck all."

John didn't want to spend any more time on that, and Morris let it go. For the first time there was a slightly uneasy atmosphere. John realised this, and made light of the situation.

"At least after a few days everyone will know who we are; they'll smell us comin' a mile off!"

"No, seriously, man, we gotta do somethin'," Gary now sounded genuinely worried.

"Let's see what's in the village," John said, to end the topic. For now. Morris said nothing. He was inside the tent, claiming his space, and deep in thought.

With everything reasonably how it should be, the four of them took their first trip into the village. A pleasant walk of only ten minutes, which was a slight surprise to the three that hadn't already had to make the journey. Their conversation included the pleasantness of the surroundings, and also about the fact that the journey back, especially the one in the dark after closing time, could be a little trickier, given the gradient.

They had also agreed that one of them should have bought some essentials, whilst they were erecting the tents. Morris took the brunt of the blame, as he had been sent to buy a mallet.

"Could've bought water and stuff whilst you were there," John stated.

"Actually, no I couldn't have." Morris defended himself. "The village shop was closed when I came down. Seems it closes at twelve."

"Is there nothing else open?" Gary asked.

"Yacht club," Morris said.

"So where'd you get the mallet from then?" John asked, realising that if there was nowhere else open, he might have stolen it.

Morris hesitated slightly, but told them he had borrowed it from a man in the marine shop, who was very friendly and only too pleased to help.

At this point, they entered the pub, except Morris, who said he was going over to thank the man for the mallet, and could they hang on to it overnight, until they can buy one.

CHAPTER SIX

It was early evening so the pub was quiet. A man who looked to be in his mid to late fifties was behind the bar placing some glasses on the shelves. As there seemed little use for bar staff at this time it didn't take a rocket scientist to work out he was the landlord. In fact, apart from an elderly gentleman sitting in the far corner of the bar, there was no one else in the pub. The lounge area was visible through the bar, and it was completely empty. The three of them approached the bar.

"You must be the three that, er, Morris is it? Has come here with?" asked the man behind the bar.

John, Gary and Eddie were taken a bit by surprise. He wasn't the brightest spark, but fair play to him, he didn't hang about when it came to making friends with pub landlords.

"Yes, that's right," John replied. Funny, he found himself ahead of the other two when they actually reached the bar. He held out his hand, and as the landlord shook it, he introduced himself and the guys.

"I'm John, and this is Gary, and Eddie."

The landlord introduced himself as he shook their hands. "I'm Rhys, Rhys Trewent. You'll find my name above the door." Immediately making the point that it was his pub, and he was the gaffer.

There followed a little friendly chat, and then with beers in hand, the three of them found a table, close to the bar, and agreed this might well be their 'spot' for the next couple of weeks.

It was important to be friendly with the landlord, and bar staff in general, so having covered the first part they would assess the 'workers' later, as they arrived for their shift. Rhys had explained that the pub never really became busy until around eight o'clock.

"And that's when Caron and Bevyn takeover," Rhys explained in his broad Welsh accent.

They had almost finished their first pint before they realised that Morris hadn't returned.

"Probably made friends with half the Marine club, or whatever it is, by now," Gary suggested. "Probably conned a drink out of someone."

As he said this, the door opened and in walked Morris. He gestured to Rhys, and walked over to the table. As he approached, Eddie spoke first.

"Introduced yourself to the rest of the village?" Morris looked a little puzzled at him.

"Well the bloody landlord knew you before we'd even set foot in the place. So we assumed you went to say 'Hi' to everyone else seeing as the population here is probably only about twenty-seven."

"Funny boy," Morris replied sarcastically. He said nothing else, but took his hand out of his jeans pocket, and dropped three keys on the table. They all looked at them, and back at Morris. To save them asking, he explained: "We each have a locker in the Yacht Club, and the use of their changing room, which includes the showers. They have our names, and you just sign in, and give the key number." The other three sat there completely stunned.

"Now, someone kindly buy me a beer before I die of thirst." And with that Morris sat down.

John looked at him with a look that said, *there's more to you than meets the eye*. John smiled as he rose from his stool and said, "This I gotta hear. How in God's name you wangled this one." He moved over to the bar.

Then came Eddie's reaction.

"Fuckin' 'ell, mate. This is brilliant!" The elation in his voice was unmistakeable. "Brilliant," he repeated, but in a whispered voice, realising the initial swearing was too loud. "How'd you do it?"

"I need a beer first." Morris stalled, and waited for John.

John returned with drinks. Once Morris had taken his first few mouthfuls, almost half the glass now empty, the questioning began.

"Well, mate. I take my hat off to you. I don't know how you pulled this one off, and I'm not entirely sure I want to know, but this is unbelievable." John was happy, but slightly unsure at the same time. How did Morris manage this? What lies has he told? Which one of us 'owns a boat', and has to know everything about sailing?

"I've hired them," Morris said. "It's no more complicated than that." He lied.

"So that's cost us how much?" Eddie asked.

"It hasn't cost you anything," Morris replied with emphasis on the 'you'. "When we decided we were going to do this, I put money aside, and this is my little contribution."

It was plausible, but John wasn't sure. The other two, however, were only too pleased to accept Morris's generosity.

"Well, mate, that's worth a few beers," Gary said. "Drinks are on us tonight, matey."

John raised his eyebrows at Gary. Then turned to Morris, "And there's another plus. These two look like they are intending to buy rounds tonight," he said, pointing at Gary and Eddie.

John wasn't going to question Morris anymore. He suspected there was more to it, but the test would be when they signed in for the first time, so no point dwelling on it now. It appeared they now had proper changing facilities. Okay, it wasn't exactly in the spirit of real camping, but no one cared, and neither did he, so just enjoy it, he thought.

And the time to test Morris's 'generosity' soon arrived. John and Gary decided they needed to shower and change before eating and drinking. Morris and Eddie couldn't be bothered, which was no surprise, so they arranged to meet back at the pub. Actually, that would be when John and Gary returned to the pub, because Morris and Eddie were going nowhere.

It was a shame they left when they did. Morris and Eddie were the first to see the bar staff, arrive behind the bar, just after 8 o'clock.

"That must be the Caron the gaffer was talking about," Eddie said.

"She's bloody lovely," Morris said with an immediate realisation that she was out of his league. They both just stared, and unfortunately for just a little bit too long.

"If you boys have a camera, I'll take a picture of her for you," boomed this heavily accented female voice across the room. "Then you wouldn't need to keep bloody starin'!"

Whilst they had been talking, and then watching the bar staff, they had failed to notice a female, of not slight proportions, walk through the door, at about the same time as the shift change, and position herself on a bar stool up against the wall separating the bar from the lounge area. They naturally looked in the direction the voice came from, and there she was, a very imposing character, staring straight at them with what could only be described as a very stern look.

She gestured towards the lady behind the bar, "Caron, you will let them have a photograph won't you? If it stops them letchin' all night."

Both parties, Morris and Eddie, and Caron, were now slightly embarrassed by the outburst. Caron glanced at the lady on the stool, and gave a wry smile.

"Fuck," Eddie said.

Morris turned toward the bar. "Sorry, didn't mean to cause offence. We are newcomers, and just takin' in the scenery." Morris figured this would break the ice and they could all laugh about it, or 'Ogre woman' would simply move across and knock them both out. It was worth finding out which was going to happen. In fact, it seemed to stun her into silence. Well, at least for a few seconds.

"She's beautiful, our Caron, but she doesn't need you two undressing her with your eyes all night."

Caron had moved round to serve someone in the lounge area, so was now unaware of the continuing conversation.

"We're just here on holiday, with a couple of other mates, and we mean no harm, so apologies if we offended anyone. I'm Morris and this is Eddie." He gestured his almost empty glass towards Eddie.

"Well, Morris and Eddie, thanks for the introduction." It wasn't a thank you at all. "I'm Myfanwy, and it would be nice to meet you, but unfortunately you're men. So as long as you stay away from me and Caron, you will live to make the journey back to wherever you came from."

Neither Morris nor Eddie heard the end of her speech. "My-fan-wee, was causing them far too much amusement. They had turned away, and were now playing 'guess the weight and age'.

"I reckon she's about thirty-five, thirty-six," guessed Morris

"What? Stone!" Eddie giggled back. It felt like they were in school, whispering at the back about the teacher, and trying not to be caught.

"You know how names usually mean something," Morris said. "I wonder what Myfanwee means?"

"Fat, loud bitch, probably," Eddie said.

The mouthful of beer Morris had just taken, was now spraying across the table, and partially over Eddie's lap. Fortunately, it wasn't in the direction of Myfanwy, and that probably saved their lives.

"Dirty bastard!" she exclaimed, giving Morris a look which could only be described as 'menacing'.

Morris was unaware of what she said, or how she was looking at him. He was too busy clearing up beer from his face, as the remainder of the mouthful had made its way down his nose, and his clothes had also taken some of the spray. Morris then made his way to the toilets, and Myfanwy turned in disgust towards the bar. She didn't need to associate herself with 'low-life' – her term for men.

John and Gary made their way back to the pub, suitably impressed with the facilities they had used at the Marine Club. They had also expected to encounter complications when they attempted to sign in, but the person on reception had been very welcoming, and it was as if they had been members for years. Neither of them could quite believe that Morris had just marched in there, and come out with members privileges. Even if he had paid for them, it was unlike him to be concerned foremost about cleanliness, and secondly, to be organised enough to sort it out. However, everything seemed to be in order on the first visit, so they both decided to accept it as one of life's strange quirks. They would not be questioning Morris any further.

As they entered the pub, they were immediately aware that business was brisker, and they looked over to see Eddie sitting on his own. John went to the bar, and Gary went over to sit with Eddie. John glanced at a slightly larger than average woman sitting on a bar stool at the bar, but didn't really acknowledge her more than that. He turned to ask Eddie if he needed a refill, and ask where Morris was.

"Yes please, mate, and Morris is in the lav. He'll need a refill too."

John turned back to face the bar, and was somewhat distracted by the very pretty woman that had come to serve him. He tried not to make it too obvious by quickly giving his drinks order. As he waited and watched, a voice from his right side seemed to be directed at him.

"So, you're with those two beasts over there then?" It wasn't the friendliest welcome he'd ever had. The tone was aggressive, and he hadn't even spoken to her. However, he didn't want to cause any problems, especially in front of a member of staff he'd quite like to be serving him his beer for the rest of the holiday.

He turned and looked at Myfanwy.

"Beasts they may be, but they're harmless," was his immediate response. He noticed that Caron was smiling, and gave him a quick glance. He smiled back, and then looked at Myfanwy.

"Don't tell me they've upset you already?" he asked.

"Taken a fancy to young Caron here," she said, gesturing with her eyes towards the barmaid.

John quickly took his opportunity. He held out his hand, first to Myfanwy (tactical, he thought). "I'm John, and yes you are stuck with us for a couple of weeks." Myfanwy shook his hand and introduced herself. As Caron put another pint on the bar, he moved his hand towards her.

"I'm John, nice to meet you," he said.

"Nice to meet you, too, I'm Caron," she almost whispered. Her voice suited her looks, soft and friendly. John guessed she was about five foot six, slight build, but not skinny. Her hair was a very dark brown, slightly wavy, and shoulder length. He thought she was probably a few years younger than him, but what attracted him most was her natural complexion. No 'excessive make-up' (although 'excessive' to him was little make-up to others), just naturally pretty. Her soft featured oval face supported high, smooth cheekbones, eyes that were wide and hazel in colour. A cute button nose, small pouty mouth that revealed perfect white teeth when she smiled. Added to her soft spoken voice and a hint of Welsh accent, John was smitten.

"Myfanwy is my bodyguard," Caron joked. "She keeps me safe, and men as far away from me as possible." She glanced at Myfanwy as she said it, but gave her a huge smile.

Myfanwy smiled back, and defended herself to John whilst still looking at Caron.

"Cheeky madam. We've been friends for many years. Don't know what you'd have done without me." The strong Welsh accent was now sounding much less aggressive, almost friendly, but John wasn't relaxing. He had quickly realised that to find out more about Caron, he needed to keep Myfanwy on his side.

"She's my rock, really," Caron confirmed, and then moved to the lounge side of the bar to serve.

John took the beers over to the table. Gary, Eddie and Morris had not missed John's reaction when first setting eyes on Caron.

"Be careful, that one there's a witch!" Morris warned him, his eyes fixed on Myfanwy. He had returned to his seat dry, and composure regained.

"No she bloody isn't," John insisted. "You just have to know how to deal with the slightly more aggressive type. It's probably just insecurity," he joked.

"You're just in love with the barmaid, mate, and would do anything to shag it," Eddie quipped.

John took exception. "Don't judge me by your standards. Does she look to you like she would be out for a 'quick shag'?" And before Eddie had chance to answer, John continued: "No," he paused. "And anyway, you'd never get passed the armed guard." He gestured towards Myfanwy, who fortunately wasn't looking.

As the evening progressed, Eddie, Morris and Gary teased John about his attraction to Caron, insisting he should get the drinks from 'his barmaid'. He didn't object to this, except for the one occasion when he was served by Bevyn. He even engaged Myfanwy in more conversation. She seemed to maintain her new found friendliness, helped by John buying her the odd G&T. Caron tried to time her availability for serving in the bar. She always talked to Myfanwy in the quieter moments anyway, but tonight she liked the banter in there, and quite liked where the banter was coming from too... one person in particular. She was trying not to let on, though.

"I don't believe you've bloody fallen for 'im already!" Myfanwy exclaimed when she caught Caron looking at John for one brief second.

Caron quickly averted her eyes, leaned towards Myfanwy, and whispered, "Not true, and will you keep your voice down. Anyway, the one that nearly shared his beer with the rest of the pub earlier, keeps looking at you. I think it's time you had a 'fancy man'." Caron smiled, and walked through to the lounge, giving no chance of reply. She heard Myfanwy say something that ended with 'never', which just made her smile more as she served the next customer.

Morris wasn't letting on, but he indeed saw some attraction in the feisty woman. He also sensed some familiarity, but couldn't put his finger on it. Anyway, he was more interested in the continuing baiting of John. John, however, reached a point where he thought they should move on to "a more interesting subject". He didn't want the rest of the holiday to revolve around him 'chasing' after female interest. He wanted to have two weeks of relaxation and fun. If that meant drinking in a pub with an attractive barmaid, so be it. If it also meant having regular banter with her 'bodyguard', that was good too. He had come on holiday with three mates and they were who he wanted to spend time with because they would take his mind off the crap situation with Jo.

They did stay for a drink after time. Rhys had appeared later in the evening, and it was all very friendly. Unfortunately, Caron and Myfanwy left once Caron had finished as they were going to eat.

As they made their way 'home' for the first time under the influence, they all agreed this had the makings of a great holiday, because the main criteria was pub and beer, and they had found both.

Eddie couldn't resist it. "And there's even a love interest already."

"I gotta be honest," John slurred slightly. "She is beautiful."

"And Caron's lovely too," Gary said. They had a few more laughs at Myfanwy's expense, but it was all good natured as she had lightened up during the course of the evening. Then they reached the bottom of the hill, and Eddie suggested a race.

"A fiver says I reach the top first." He was looking for a taker.

"If I ran up there, you'd spend the rest of the night clearing out my puke from our tent," Gary informed him.

There were no takers, but Eddie 'ran' up it anyway. They knew when he had reached the top, they could hear him being sick over the wall.

"That must have been a dodgy pint, that last one." Eddie tried to defend himself from the suggestions that he could no longer hold his beer.

They approached their 'base' only whispering, and with some trepidation. None of them sure why, it was just a natural reaction to knowing they shouldn't be there. What if someone was waiting behind the wall to move them on? Or if they made too much noise, someone would be bound to hear them. They didn't want to have to pack up in the middle of the night, drunk and nowhere to go!

It was very dark when they entered the field. "Where did you leave the torch?" John continued to whisper.

"In the shop," Morris said casually.

"Brilliant, so we don't have any means of light," John said.

Eddie lit a cigarette and held his lighter up. The breeze blew it out in an instant, so he flicked it on again, holding his other hand round it as a shield. John then held up the torch on his phone. "Good thinking" said Gary, realising they all had that facility. They managed to get themselves in to their respective tents, and once in, their phone lights created some interesting shadows, as they settled down for the night. Morris then decided he needed a pee, and in fact they all decided that was a good idea. One o'clock in the morning they are all spread out along the wall of the field, doing their best not to pee on themselves, or each other.

Finally settled, there was a small amount of conversation in each tent, but silence eventually fell. John was not particularly comfortable, but the evenings alcohol consumption, soon began to take its effect. As he drifted off, suddenly, from Morris's direction, came the loudest passing of wind John had ever heard. And it lasted for a good few seconds. Loud laughter ensued, with applause also coming from the other tent.

"Jesus Christ!" John yelled out, as he fought to release himself from his sleeping bag.

Another one followed quickly, then another one. "Oh yeah!" Morris called out in satisfaction of their release.

"Oh fuck that stinks." John was grasping at the zip of the tent. Huge laughter continued from the other tent.

"Enough man. Jesus!" John at least got his head outside. Then he managed to scramble out completely.

Another one. A few seconds silence, and then another one. The stillness of the beautiful Welsh countryside, broken only by the distant sound of the sea, lapping ashore and Morris's wind.

"Don't you shit yourself in there!" John called out. "I get the fuckin' fartie pants!" he remonstrated out loud.

Laughter continued from the other tent.

Morris stuck his head outside. He couldn't see John at first, so he just spoke, knowing he was there somewhere. "Sorry, mate. It must be the local beer. Can't see you, but I'm coming out. Need to find my lighter."

"Don't light that bugger in there!" John joked.

Morris had stuck his head back in the tent, and was fumbling around for his lighter. John heard him get out.

"Better leave these flaps open a bit. Sticking my head back in there, it does smell a bit like someone's shit themselves."

"Someone!" John exclaimed. Then pleaded, "No more, please."

Someone had opened the other tent. It was Eddie, still finding the whole event very amusing,

"It's a bloody good job we're the only people on this 'campsite'. You'd have woken the whole neighbourhood."

As Morris stood, smoking his cigarette, Eddie came over to light his. Morris let out another. John and Eddie moved away quickly.

"That's it. I can't go back in there. It'll be like sleeping in a shit house." John was trying to sound angry, but sounded as though he was holding back laughter.

Eddie had let out another burst of laughter.

"Bloody hell, man. You are gonna shit yourself in a minute."

"No, no, I'm fine. Think it's done now," Morris said.

John gave it a good few minutes before returning to the tent. Even then, he didn't actually climb back in until Morris had sworn he wouldn't unleash anymore.

From the other tent came a warning from Gary, "That's alright whilst he's still awake. Has no control once he's asleep!"

John, laying in his sleeping bag, turned away from Morris to face the side of the tent. As he turned, he was heard to say, "That's what I'm worried about... probably wake up next to a pile of shit!"

The laughter died down, and soon there was just the distant sound of waves. And a short, loud rasp of wind.

CHAPTER SEVEN

The first morning was a memorable one for John. The aroma suggested either a herd of cattle had used this corner of the field as their dumping ground, or perhaps more likely, Morris had farted his way through the night. One thing was for sure, he had to open that zip and find fresh air from somewhere.

After clambering out of the tent, and noticing immediately that there were no livestock, or any of their deposits within sight, and that the air was clear and fresh, Morris was clearly the culprit. Two weeks of that was going to be a challenge. John stood and looked out over the surrounding scenery. The sun was shining, and this was quite definitely a beautiful part of the world. Although the trees on the opposite side of the road to the field partly blocked the view, he could see a small field below, leading to a sandy looking beach, and the sea.

As he stood taking all this in, it occurred to him that the zip to the tent had been half open when he ventured out. *Where was Morris?* he wondered. He stuck his head back through the entrance. No, not there. He stood upright, and looked over the field and the surrounding area. No sign of him. Perhaps he was in the other tent. He looked at his watch and thought perhaps he had slept late, and the others gone somewhere; although after last night's events, it was doubtful Eddie and Gary would have let him in. Anyhow, it was only eight thirty, so that hardly constituted sleeping late. There was no sound coming from the other tent, but he walked up to it. As he approached, it was obvious the other two were still asleep, but he 'knocked' on the front of the tent, which of course made virtually no sound.

"Anyone awake yet?" he called out.

A barely audible grumble came from within, and then silence. So John left them, and turned his attention back to where Morris could possibly be. Actually, there wasn't much Morris could be doing. He thought it was out of character, but decided that Morris must have gone to the club for a shower.

It was not long before life emerged from the other tent, and after some re-capping of the previous night's entertainment, certain disbelief from Gary and Eddie that Morris must have risen early to shower, they were themselves ready for the walk to the club.

Caron and Myfanwy had spent their evening having a late meal, and a few drinks at Myfanwy's house, discussing the merits or pitfalls of a holiday romance. The subject had arisen because of the conversation about the 'newcomers'. Caron admitted that, on first impressions, she had been taken with John.

"But you know nothing about him, and every man who walks through that door fancies you, so you hold the balance of power. Remember that."

Myfanwy's view of men was very one sided. She was in love once, until he broke her heart and left her for someone else. She suspected he had been seeing "the other woman" for some time, and this had scared her. She would never admit it to anyone, other than Caron. She just hid her own bad experience behind a very stern exterior, and generalised that men were not to be trusted. She had been single for some time now, and at thirty-eight, had taken Caron 'under her wing' to 'protect' her.

Caron was thirty-two years old, and had a very trusting outlook on life. She had experienced a couple of "not so happy ending" relationships herself, and Myfanwy stepped in after the second. But that was a year ago, and whilst she enjoyed the life she had, sometimes it would be nice to share good times with a male companion. This was the part that Myfanwy guarded against.

"A holiday romance isn't going to give you the companionship longer term, though, is it? In fact, you'll barely have time to remember his name, and he'll be off.

And I bet he's married. Won't mention that, though, will he? No, he'll be like all of them… see an opportunity, take what he can, and then, thanks. Bye!"

"You can be so bitter sometimes," Caron replied. "You don't know he's like that. Yes, he could be married." She shrugged her shoulders, "But I can't go through life judging people before I give them a chance. And there are at least a few good people in this world… maybe he's one of them? Besides, he might not be interested. He's here on holiday with three mates, and anyway, I only said he was good looking and seemed nice. Doesn't mean I want him to sweep me of my feet." There was a short silence, as they maintained eye contact. "Although," Caron added, smiling, "That would be nice."

"If he knows you're interested, he'll be interested."

"Well, he won't know I'm interested, will he," Caron emphasised. "Unless I choose to drop a few subtle hints." She paused. "Maybe I could ask him to be my date for David's party tomorrow night?" She smiled, as she knew that would get a reaction.

"Very subtle. More like, 'Come with me, as I'm really interested in you,' is what that says." Myfanwy replied.

Caron laughed. "As if I would do that; perhaps I'll just sleep with him." Myfanwy realised she was being wound up, and they laughed that suggestion off.

Myfanwy's facial expression had changed, and Caron knew she was about to hear motherly advice.

"Be careful, though, my love. And remember I'm always here for you."

Caron put her hand on Myfanwy's, "Thanks, mum," she whispered.

"Don't take the piss now." Myfanwy warned, as she clasped Caron's hand.

"No, I know, and thank you. But you are making it sound like I'm about to venture into the unknown, and the likelihood is, nothing will happen. This is me just having some 'perfect world' time."

Caron returned home that night hoping the guys would be there the following evening. They would probably be up for a party too. David wouldn't mind. He invited everyone he met.

Myfanwy went to bed wondering which one it was she did actually take a bit of a liking to, Morris or Eddie, as she wasn't sure she had the names round the right way. But she would sort it out, without letting on to anyone.

Arriving at the club, Gary signed in first, and above his signature was that of Morris.

"He's here, look." Gary moved the book towards the others.

"I don't understand: one, why he would get up so early, and two, how he didn't wake everyone else up in the process. He can hardly be called Mr Considerate, but he didn't even disturb me, and I was right next to him." John remained puzzled as they made their way to the changing rooms.

"To be fair, you had been gassed," Gary pointed out.

They found Morris, who was indeed, in the shower. Something else was going on with Morris, in John's opinion. Even if he had only just left when John woke up, that was nearly an hour ago and he was only just showering? Where had he been? John chose to think no more of it for now.

Eddie switched the showers' mains hot water off, as they were getting undressed, and waited a few seconds. Morris's wailing, as his nice hot shower suddenly turned ice cold, could be heard from a distance!

To add to John's thoughts about Morris, it was noted, that Morris was strangely subdued throughout much of the day. Gary observed it at one point, mentioning it to John, but having both acknowledged it, they decided if there was a problem, Morris would tell them eventually, and anyway, they were probably looking for something that wasn't there.

Their second evening began normally. Morris had found an excuse to get to the pub early, so when the others arrived he was already in deep conversation with an unsuspecting member of the public.

His name was Dave, and it was immediately clear that Morris had found a like-minded friend, as they were discussing the effects of beer on bodily functions. John was quick to warn Morris.

"I will kick your arse out the tent tonight if you repeat last night's performance," he said.

John, Gary and Eddie were in the process of introducing themselves to Dave, who invited them back to his house later that evening for a bit of a bash once the pub closed. So another master stroke had been pulled by Morris – now he had found them a party. To make the whole evening look like it was going to be complete, Myfanwy and Caron made it clear that they were fully intent on partying after closing time too. John didn't want to make any assumptions, but as the evening went on, he and Caron seemed to 'connect', so he was hopeful he might get to know Caron a little better once she didn't have to keep 'running off' to serve people. Morris and Myfanwy seemed to engage in playful verbal abuse, which Caron had observed. "We could be witnessing something special between those two," she said.

John replied, "Does she date men or lure them to her place, and eat them?"

"Yes, it's possible she could do that." Caron pondered. "But I have to say I've never seen her verbally abuse someone, and then carry on talking to them. Morris obviously enjoys it?"

"Positively relishes it, it would seem," John agreed.

As closing time approached, Dave and a few of his mates who had arrived during the course of the evening, decided it was time to leave and make sure the house was open and ready for 'business' once the pub closed. Morris agreed to help too. Dave had invited everyone who set foot in the pub that evening, including a man who came round selling the latest DVDs and CDs.

"Is he a mate of yours?" Eddie asked Gary, as they looked through the merchandise.

"Very funny." Gary was dismissive. "Nothin' dodgy about my business," he insisted, unconvincingly.

Morris was heard to 'quietly' enquire if Myfanwy was still intending to come to the party as he left. The other three nudged each other as they noticed Morris making his polite inquiry. Smiles all round. Could Morris be in love? John cast his eyes to behind the bar where Caron was standing, and Morris started to walk away from Myfanwy. She glanced over, raised her eyes, smiled, and mouthed "told you" as she gestured towards them. John smiled back, felt quite good himself, and watched Morris walk towards the door.

Morris turned to the lads, "I'm checking it out, boys. If you hear nothing, then assume it's okay to come over." He left.

"That's not necessarily gonna be the case, is it?" Gary paused. "It could just mean he's lyin' pissed in a corner somewhere."

John turned to Gary and Eddie, and whispered, "He ain't gonna get 'mullered' is he?" As he said this, he was gesturing his eyes in the general direction of Myfanwy.

"Do you really think he wants to shag that?" Eddie was also gesturing towards Myfanwy.

"Ow! Fuckin' hell!" Eddie screamed.

Nobody had a chance to answer, or even move, before Eddie was being dragged from his stool by his hair. His stool crashed to the floor; he caught the table as he was being dragged, which caused beer glasses and beer to disperse over it and the floor. John and Gary shot off their stools, fortunately without catching much of the cascading beer, and quickly moved to the other side of the room.

Eddie was now on his feet, but standing like a scolded school boy with teacher holding his ear, against one of the oak pillars in the middle of the room. Only 'teacher' had a good handful of his hair gripped tightly in her hand.

Eddie's face was screwed up and a feeble sounding, "Get off, that fuckin' hurts, woman," came out as he held his hands up to his head.

"Now then," Myfanwy said through gritted teeth. "Who wants to shag who?"

"I was only having a laugh" Eddie said, still with pain written on his face.

Myfanwy let go of his hair and pushed Eddie away at the same time. His head hit the pillar.

"Ow, bollocks!" Eddie exclaimed.

"Good job you were only jokin' and I was only mucking about then." Myfanwy looked at Caron, then looked back at Eddie. "Because I can get aggressive when I'm angry!" Myfanwy walked off to the toilet.

John and Gary had sat down whilst this was going on, and watched the entertainment with considerable amusement. Eddie smiled as he joined them, but was still rubbing his head.

"She's a bit quick of the mark," John said.

"And for a fat cow, moves a bit quick too," Eddie said.

The three of them were laughing, but John had a slight concern that if Myfanwy really had been upset by it, she may decide not to go to the party, and that might mean Caron wouldn't either. So he was somewhat relieved when having gone up to the bar to buy drinks, Caron smiled and let him know that it was just Myfanwy's way of letting everyone know she was in control as she didn't want people to think she was softening just because she happened to like someone.

"I don't want to be around when she doesn't like someone then," John said.

"No, you don't," Caron replied smiling. John confirmed to himself, that Caron was really quite beautiful, which in turn started to cast his own doubts as to why she would be interested in him.

As closing time approached, John found himself experiencing a few nerves. Despite telling himself there was nothing to be nervous about, he also felt as though his behaviour had changed. He was back at school, in the classroom thinking about the girl he was going to ask out on the way home.

"This is ridiculous," he told himself. But when Caron rang for last orders, he felt so incredibly nervous; he thought everyone must realise what his plan was.

His plan? He didn't even have one. He didn't even know if Caron was still going, and someone else may have started to chat her up in the other bar. He didn't know who was in there, or what had been going on. *Jesus, just listen to yourself*, he thought. *Get a fuckin' grip, and stop this nonsense*. After a moment's pause, he did have to admit to himself, that no one had made him feel like this for as long as he could remember. That made him smile.

"Are you guys going to wait for me and Myfanwy?" Now there was a question John thought he'd never hear. There was an uncomfortable gap, before he came out of his semi-dazed state, and turned to see Caron smiling at him.

"Or you could pretend you never heard me, and just leave," she said before he had chance to reply.

"Yes," he said.

"Yes, you'll just leave?" She paused. "Hello," she said softly. "Is there anyone there?"

Immediately, he refocused and looked her straight in the eye. "Sorry, of course I'll…" he corrected himself. "We'll wait."

The guys stood outside for a while waiting for the girls. Myfanwy and Eddie had 'made up', which actually meant that Eddie had apologised, several times, and a man grovelling did have a remarkably calming effect on Myfanwy. Rarely could she be accused of admiring a man, except for once when one tried to recruit her into the local BNP Party with the reasoning that they needed strong, forceful members who could run the country. She knew he was drunk, she had no tendencies towards the BNP, and even she had no desire to run the country, but nevertheless, it did stop her from putting his head through the pub wall, and that meant some sort of respect.

The bar door opened and Caron and Myfanwy appeared in the semi-darkness, the outside light provided very little visibility, but enough to bring John's nerves back. He was excited too. Just to be in the position of trying to win over a woman's affections seemed a strange thing for a man of his age to be doing, but he had a good feeling about it, although he didn't plan on what the remainder of the night had in store for him.

CHAPTER EIGHT

It was only a short walk up to where Dave's house was, and even for John, Gary and Eddie, it would have been easy to find, had they not been with the girls, all they had to do was follow the music. Actually, in a place the size of Dale, nothing was very far. On the way, they passed Caron's house, Myfanwy's house, and although they didn't know it, they passed the properties of just about everyone who was attending the party. Dave had invited the neighbourhood and it was apparent, given the volume level of the music, that no one in the village would sleep very much anyway.

The house was above road level. It had a four foot drop at the end of the front garden. The front lawn was split down the centre by the steps which led up from road level, and the path that took you to the front door. The front door was wide open. People were standing on the front lawn, drinking, chatting, and laughing. As the new arrivals entered the house, 'Sultans of Swing' was playing.

Gary turned to John, "Musically, I'm liking it so far," he said. John was in to music, but it wasn't really his main focus for this evening. Eddie had already disappeared into the back garden, beer in hand and searching for Morris.

John, Gary, Caron and Myfanwy all headed straight for the kitchen. Caron had bought a couple of bottles of wine from the pub, at "staff negotiated rates" as she put it, and John had also acquired a dozen bottles of beer from the pub, as he took advantage of staff rates. The other three hadn't felt the need to suggest taking drink with them as they knew John wouldn't let them down. Many people were saying "Hi" to Myfanwy and Caron, as they all threaded their way through.

Once they were in the kitchen, John noticed that a number of people, mainly male, had followed them in there, and the greetings continued, whilst John and Gary helped themselves to a beer. Caron and Myfanwy had already been given wine glasses, and a bottle wine, so they didn't need any assistance.

Dave appeared, and greeted the guys as though they had been mates for years. In a house full of people that you have never met before, that was what John and Gary needed, because the onslaught of people who took Caron and Myfanwy's attention away, meant the two could have felt very isolated, very quickly.

Dave wanted to know all about why they had come to Dale, how long for, and where they were staying. However, due to the pace at which Dave obviously lived his life, he wanted to know it all in less than a minute. His attention span also seemed to be working in tandem, because during that frantic minute he spoke to at least four other people, and asked them how they were. Resisting the temptation to tell Dave that they were all in fact ex-convicts who had an addiction to entering house parties and stealing anything valuable, John decided to make his excuses, and try to find Eddie and Morris. Dave wouldn't have heard his sarcasm anyway, so he saved his breath.

John took his opportunity to 'escape' as Dave welcomed another guest. He gestured to Gary, but he had started a conversation with another person who had been introduced, John had already forgotten his name.

So John made his way out of the kitchen, he looked over to Caron, and she was engrossed in conversation with her own little crowd. He fought his way out to the back garden, but couldn't immediately see Eddie or Morris. He wandered down the lawn, it looked quite a big back garden. It was dark, and the lights from the house only lit up the first few yards. He could make out the red glows of cigarette ends, and they were still quite a few yards away.

He wandered a short distance down, and as he did, he kept an eye out for Eddie and Morris. But they had obviously moved and found something to amuse them elsewhere in the house.

John suddenly felt alone. These feelings crept up on him unawares just lately. He looked up to the night sky, which he noticed was very clear, and tried to work out why, in the middle of a lively party, on a holiday with three mates who were proving to be a good laugh, he felt like this. At this point he thought about Jo for the first time since they had been away. He had come away to at least try and put her out of his head for a couple of weeks. Although he never believed he could do that, at least he might have the chance to be a little more relaxed about the whole situation, and having a break might help put it all into perspective. So he smiled to himself, as he realised it had taken but just two days to come back and "beat him over the head". But he began to wonder what she was doing now. She'd probably had a good day by the pool and getting tanned. Life was on the up for her, and she would be happy and safe, which was at least some comfort to him.

This wasn't the only reason for his sudden change of mood. Being honest with himself, he had thought a night in the company of Caron would help put it to the back of his mind for a few hours. To have arrived at the party, and immediately 'lost' her to other people was frustrating, however, not totally unexpected. After all, this was her home town, or village, whatever it was classed as. *Enjoy the evening, and take it for what it is… stop over-thinking stuff.*

Caron was an attractive woman with an infectious personality. He had been here 'five minutes', she had grown up here. Whatever made him think that within the space of two visits to the pub, half a dozen exchanged words, and a walk to a party, she would walk, unchallenged, and into his life? He answered his own question; the natural male thought process that's what. Truth was, he had no right. She could probably have the pick of any man here, so to think that it would suddenly be him, he was kidding himself. Caron's very nature seemed to be friendly, and that's what she had been. Besides, life was a succession of choices and priorities. His priority, and without question, his choice, was to make things right with Jo, because without that relationship there were no choices or priorities, so anything else paled into insignificance. When he returned from this holiday, he would sort everything out with her. He would never be happy with the move, but it had happened and he had to accept it, and he couldn't let it get in the way. With that positive thought in his mind, it was time to refocus, and move on with the holiday, find the lads, and get pissed.

He became aware, once again of the party going on around him, and made his way back in to the house. It was time for another beer, the first one having taken him far too long. The kitchen was 'heaving', so he fought his way over to get a drink and looked over to where Caron had been standing. She wasn't there. Then he spotted Gary, who seemed to be deeply engrossed in conversation with a female. Rather than cramp him, John decided it was time to find Eddie and Morris. He tried not to wonder where Caron had got to, but found himself looking for her as well. As he forced his way through the hallway and into one of two lounges, he saw her talking with two guys, and Myfanwy. They were laughing, drinking and generally having a good time which, is what you would expect people at a party to do, but of course, he didn't like that it wasn't with him. John turned and walked into the second lounge across the hall.

As John left the room, a pair of eyes followed him out. How had they become separated so quickly, and where had he been? Got to manoeuvre out of this conversation, which is boring anyway, and catch up with proper company, thought Caron.

As John entered the second room, he decided he wasn't going to be purely dependant on finding the other guys for conversation, so he introduced himself to a group of three girls and one guy standing talking about who knows what. But they had looked at him as he entered, and that was a good enough excuse to break the ice.

"Hi," he said, as he held out his hand to each one. "I'm John, here on holiday with three other misfits who are scattered around the place." That sounded a bit naff, but it was the only thing he could think to say.

"We're on holiday too. Hi, I'm Katie."

"Hi, Katie." John had been told once that the best way to remember people's names, was to repeat it after they had told you it.

"Hannah."

"Hi, Hannah."

"Hi, I'm Amy."

"Hi, Amy."

"And I'm Josh, Katie's Husband, and Hannah and Amy's brother."

"Hi, Josh." If Josh hadn't actually repeated the girls' names again, he would have all but forgotten them already. Proving to himself that no 'trick' in the book could ever hide the fact that he considered himself to have the worst memory anybody could ever have. They seemed very friendly, and in the brief few minutes of their meeting, John decided he liked them and that they seemed to like him. He wasn't so alone now, he had made new friends.

However, after only a few moments of their introductions, a very distressed girl came running into the house, from the front door. As she passed down the hallway, she could be heard calling out,

"Somebody has just fallen off the wall at the front," she said. "Someone call an ambulance. I think he's out cold!"

She'd had to run into the house to give the order to call 999 because the area wasn't known for its fantastic mobile signal, no matter what provider. John had realised a little earlier in the garden, when it crossed his mind to try calling Jo. He looked down to see a blank line, where the signal strength should be.

As someone went for the phone, or rather, to ask Dave where the phone was, a number of people headed for the front door. Generally, the news had been met with a certain amount of hilarity. Most people were at the slightly drunk stage, some were beyond that, and as John was soon to find out, some had gone way beyond even that.

John and his new friends turned towards the lounge door, and that human instinct of follow the crowd sort of kicked in. For John, however, there was a very uneasy feeling. Something inside told him to get down to the bottom of that front garden, because he was needed. As he walked towards the front door he actually started to push past people, and found himself moving very quickly down to the top of the wall.

As he looked down, there were two things that hit him. One, the person was absolutely out cold, and two… *Oh my God, it's Eddie*, he realised. "Oh fuck!" he said. Eddie was motionless.

John was momentarily stunned by what he was looking at, and for those first few seconds, didn't move. He had to comprehend in his own mind, what literally lay before him.

"Oh, crap, this is my mate Eddie," John said. "Has someone phoned for an ambulance?" He wasn't addressing anyone in particular, just generally to the crowd of people, and as he said it, he knew someone had because of the initial commotion inside the house.

Somebody did answer him anyway, with a "Yes", and on hearing that, John knew he had to find Gary and Morris. In fact he couldn't understand why they hadn't come to find out what all the fuss was about. However, he needed to check Eddie first, so he moved quickly down the steps to road level, and knelt down by him. He called his name but there was no response. He needed to see or feel he was breathing, for his own satisfaction, before trying to find the other two. He put his face up to Eddie's mouth and nose, whilst checking for a pulse.

"It's okay, he's breathing, I checked," someone said.

He stood up and said to no one in particular that he had to find his two other mates, and asked people to keep an eye on Eddie. He ran up the front garden, which was clear of people because they were all now either looking over the edge, or standing down on the road level, staring at an unconscious stranger. Into the house he went poking his head into each room in his search. There were a surprising number of people still in the house, who seemed oblivious as to what was going on outside. Most, if not all, seemed to be very loud and drunk, so it wasn't difficult to work out why they had no idea anything had happened.

As he looked into the kitchen, there was Gary leaning up against the fridge freezer, talking to the same girl he had left him with. So he quickly walked over to him and grabbed his arm.

"Gary, there's been an accident. Eddie's knocked himself out..." he had no chance to say any more. Gary looked at him, and attempted to stand up straight.

"He should wait, because I'm just a bit busy right now," he said.

"Wait for what?" John replied, knowing that this was a totally pointless question, and in fact, as he stared at Gary's face, and Gary's face was swaying in time with the rest of his body, eyes half-closed, John decided there was no point trying to explain anything else to him and turned to leave.

"Never mind," he said as he turned. He had to find Morris, Gary wasn't going to be of any use.

The last he saw of Morris was in the back garden. That was at least an hour ago, and Morris was quite visibly unstable then. So, fearing the worst, he quickly ran out the back. As he did so he heard a siren. The ambulance was arriving, and he quickly had to check what he had already resigned himself to, that Morris would be similar to Gary and be in no fit state to understand what was happening.

As he approached the body lying face down on the lawn, his fears were about to be confirmed. He called "Morris" as he looked down. There was a short but incoherent grunt of recognition, but as the ground around about the body seemed a bit wet and there was an unpleasant aroma, John decided that leaving Morris lying in his own vomit might be best for now. Morris did make an attempt to lift his head and turn, but John didn't have time to wait, nor did he really want to see the true state Morris was in, that was the least of his problems right now.

The siren was now much louder, as John ran back into the house. As he made his way to the front door, passing the kitchen, there stood Caron, holding a mug out in his direction. He looked at her.

"I thought you might need black coffee," she offered. In her way she was trying to show John she wanted to help, but didn't quite know what to do.

John did stop for a brief second, as the siren was now quite definitely outside the house.

"Thanks, but I'm okay," he said raising half a smile. Why did she have to do this? That would start him thinking about her again, and he was likely to have to leave for the evening in an ambulance. Besides, he'd made a definite decision to put those feelings to one side, enjoy the holiday and concentrate on making things good with Jo. *Damn Caron for doing this. Why can't she just be a horrible person?*

"If you need me to help," she added, as her eyes followed him to the front door, "then I want to," she said softly, because John had left.

The paramedics were attending to Eddie, as John returned to where he lay. He explained who he was, and they gave him an assessment.

"There appears to be a fracture in his right wrist, and he has concussion." There was a pause.

"What?" exclaimed John, agitated. He was looking for some encouragement that Eddie was going to be ok.

"Well we are more concerned about his pupils being dilated," explained one.

"And what does that mean?" John was trying to remain calm.

"Well, it could be just the fact that he's had quite a lot of alcohol, but it could also mean a head injury. But we need to get him to hospital before we can really tell."

"Shit! Okay, well I'm coming with you," John said.

"Yes, that's fine." Replied the paramedic.

A sudden wave of realisation passed through John, and he wasn't ready for it. As Eddie lay in the ambulance, air mask over his mouth, John stared at him, as he was having great difficulty believing this was happening. The ambulance was making its way through the Welsh country lanes, blue lights flashing, and its siren disturbing an otherwise peaceful late evening.

The journey to hospital took almost half an hour during which time Eddie had opened his eyes briefly, mumbled something, and closed them again. The paramedic explained what they would do at the hospital, and gave John some comfort by giving him all the reasons why she was sure Eddie would be okay. On arrival he jumped out and followed the medical staff, as they took Eddie into a room to start their work on him. A nurse took John to a waiting room, and told him someone would update him as soon as they could.

It was now two thirty in the morning, and John sat alone trying to comprehend what was happening here. It even made him smile, as he put his head in his hands. This wasn't quite what he had planned for this evening – a few drinks in the pub, wander over to a party, have a few more drinks with his mates, get to know a beautiful woman a little better, meet some new people… still sounded great. Reality – few drinks, wander to a party, lose his mates immediately, spend time alone in the garden, not even speak to a beautiful woman, and the only people he got to know better were two paramedics, as they took one of his mates to hospital, unsure, however, as to whether or not he had serious head injuries. Now, he was sitting in a hospital waiting room at two thirty in the morning. Surely it couldn't get any worse?

And for a while it didn't. A doctor eventually came to advise him that Eddie was going to be fine.

"He will probably feel a bit groggy in the morning, but that'll be more due to the effects of drinking than anything to do with his accident. He has fractured his right wrist, so we've put it in plaster."

It was a huge relief for John to hear that Eddie was okay, and he greeted the news of the broken wrist with a smile. Piss taking would be the result of this fiasco, and nothing more than that. The doctor, however, didn't seem to share John's amusement, and noticing the 'relaxed' attitude, stared straight at John and stated with some authority, "Because there was a suspected head injury, we will keep him here for at least another twenty-four hours, but then he should be fine to go." John realised the stern Welsh voice contained slight annoyance in it. There was a slight pause, then the doctor continued: "So, the best thing you can do is go home. Maybe come back tomorrow, when your friend will be awake, and probably embarrassed."

John decided not to enter into any further conversation. It was probably better to leave. To be fair, he thought, patching up drunk people every night, must get a bit tedious.

"Cool. Okay, well I probably need a cab, so do you have a number I could call?" John was now beginning to realise that in relation to where their tents were pitched, he didn't really know where he was, or how far away they were. The ambulance journey hadn't given him any help. He wasn't exactly gazing out of the window during it, and in any case the sheer darkness of the night made it impossible to reference any landmarks that they might have passed. As they hadn't seemed to pass any street lighting, until they were almost at the hospital, John assumed most of the journey had been through countryside, so late night buses or trains probably weren't going to be an option.

"I doubt you will get a cab at this time of night," The doctor replied. "We're not quite the size of London." And with that, the doctor turned and left the room.

Almost before the door closed, and John had had time to realise he was alone once again, the door re-opened, and in walked two policemen.

"Good evening, sir."

"Hello," John said, confused as to why he was now presumably going to be questioned by these two officers. He momentarily saw them, with 'Taxi' written above their head, but thought best to hear what they had to say first.

"Your mate," one of them began. "Been on drugs has he?"

Jesus! John quickly realised they were being serious, after glancing quickly at each officer.

"What?" he exclaimed, at a volume he didn't intend, but nevertheless caused a reaction from the officers

"All right, sir. If we just keep our voices down, then we won't disturb anybody at this late hour."

John glanced at the clock on the wall above the door. Just after 3am. And now he was about to be interrogated as to whether or not his mate was a crack head.

"Three o'clock in the morning, my mate's lying in a hospital bed, and I can't get back to the others. I have no fuckin' idea where I am," John said sharply, but one of the officers didn't let him finish.

"Sir, sit down please." The tone was friendly, but had the more authority.

John sat down, realising he should calm down, this really wasn't as bad as he was making out. The officer spoke again, before John could offer an apology.

"Your mate, from what we can establish, was at the party and ran down the garden, straight over the wall, and on to the road." He paused. John didn't say anything, just continued to look at the floor. *The party*, sounded as if the officers knew which party, so had they been there? It didn't surprise him that they knew which party, but it did mean that perhaps they would be going back that way, so co-operation and calmness was probably wise.

The officer continued, "According to the doctor, there was evidence of him being under the influence of alcohol and perhaps drugs."

John looked up, "Well, I'm sure there are tests you can do, but I can assure you Eddie was just good old-fashioned pissed." He finished the sentence with half a smile on his face, it was the best he could do. He was tired, and didn't know how he was getting 'home'.

"Yes, they did have to tidy him up a bit, take blood and all that, but we won't know any results until the morning."

John looked at the officers, and not wanting to agitate them, but also wanting to make his point, simply said, "You have to do what you have to do, I understand that. But you are wasting your time. Eddie just sees an opportunity to party and get drunk. It's really no more complicated than that."

The officers also realised that there was probably very little in this, but there was a process they had to follow. They stood up and simply stated that they would call by in the morning, and suggested John go home.

John seized the moment, "Actually, I'm not sure where that is from here." It was purposely toned as a question, because of his ulterior motive. He stood because it made him feel less like he was about to beg.

"It's quite easy really," came the reply. "It's only about thirteen miles, and two roads. Pretty straight forward."

"And at this time of night, I do that journey, how?" John said sarcastically.

There was a slight pause. Mainly because as John was speaking, a man entered the room. A cleaner, or someone who wasn't a doctor anyway, was all John could make out. The officers exchanged pleasantries with him, and then turned their attention back to John. "You may find a cab, but unlikely. Is there anyone who could come and pick you up?" asked one officer.

"As I left, one was having trouble stringing two words together, and the other one was head down in his own vomit, so they are probably just over the limit by now," he said this with a smile on his face because he felt they were being a little ridiculous to think that having come from a party, someone would now drive to pick him up. But he didn't want to antagonise them, so he wanted them to know he wasn't being serious. Both officers seem to take the point, so whist the 'cleaner', who the officers had greeted as Martin, went about his duties, John went for it.

"Are you not going back that way?"

"No, mate, sorry," replied one. "Not a lot of call for police in Dale at this time of night." He paused. "Or ever, actually, thank God. Take care now." And the officers left the room.

"Fuck. What do I do now?" John asked himself, realising that sitting in this room for the night was becoming a real possibility.

"Where you got to get to, mate?" Martin asked, who John had momentarily forgotten was still in the room.

"Dale," he replied

Martin stood up from where he was kneeling down next to the TV, fixing whatever it was, to do with the plug.

"Let me go and ask Ewan. He lives that way, and finishes his shift at seven thirty. Might be able to give you a lift." Martin hesitated, waiting for a reaction from John. All John could think of was that seven thirty was still four hours away. There's only so many 'OK' and 'Hello' magazines you can read in one sitting, and four hours' worth was stretching it a bit.

"Oh great, that would be helpful, thanks." The guy, was only trying to help, and that in itself was quite refreshing. So without thinking any further, John accepted the offer.

Martin left the room, and John sat back down. He looked round the room, and whilst doing so, thought about just how badly the evening had gone. He thought about Jo, and he wanted to talk to her right now, but at this time of night, that wouldn't really help him patch things up. Caron?, well that had gone completely 'pear shaped', so no point dwelling on that he told himself, so he dwelt on it for a while longer. She had many friends at the party, and she had known him for five minutes. He mentally shook himself, and instead of going over the same thing, leant over to the small table and picked up a copy of 'OK' magazine. Time to look at pictures of celebrities, in their fancy homes.

After only about ten minutes, John could hear two voices approaching, and seconds later the door opened. In came Martin, followed by presumably, Ewan.

Martin introduced the two, "This is Gareth." And Martin then looked at John, and hesitated because of course, he had no idea what John's name was. So he turned towards Gareth, and said "And this is the bloke I was telling you about."

John was a bit confused. Where was Ewan, whoever he was, and where did Gareth come into the equation? John, nevertheless, held out his hand and introduced himself to Gareth. Martin then clarified, "Ewan's ill apparently, so Gareth has taken his shift. Luckily, Gareth lives near Ewan, so he goes the same way home."

John turned his attention to Gareth, but before he could say anything, Gareth asked him, "Where is it you need to get to?"

John was a bit confused, and beginning to doubt the whole validity of this. "Dale," he replied, wondering how these two had had a conversation, about his need to get home, at three-thirty in the morning, without mentioning where it was he needed to go?

"Oh, okay. I can drop you there when I finish, no problem. I finish at seven-thirty, is that okay?"

John wasn't in any position to argue. "Perfect," he replied. "I'm gonna try and close my eyes for an hour or so, I'm knackered." He added. Noticing just two plastic chairs in the room, however, he wasn't convinced any sleep was coming his way.

"Tell you what," Martin sounded like he'd just had the best idea ever. "I'll take you to our porter's room. There's a sofa you could sleep on, and I can get you a couple of blankets."

Without even seeing it yet, it sounded the better option to John. Any kind of sofa had to be more comfortable than a couple of plastic chairs.

The porter's room wasn't 'five star', but the sofa was inviting, as long as he didn't look at the stains on the cushion covers for too long. Martin had left the room, but returned quickly with a pillow and two blankets. He had taken them from the laundry room and he did stress they were from the freshly laundered pile. John did have a sneaky smell of them as Martin handed them over, but to John, everything in a hospital smelt the same, and in any event he was too tired to care that much, so he thanked Martin, and prepared his 'bed'.

"Gareth will be leaving about seven-thirty, so he'll come and get you then," Martin reminded him and left the room.

John took his shoes off, threw the pillow to one end of the sofa, grabbed the blankets, and lay on the sofa. As his head touched the pillow, he closed his eyes. Things were going to be okay. Eddie was fine, and he himself, would be back in Dale by eight in the morning.

As the ambulance pulled away, lights flashing, Caron felt alarmed at what had just happened. She liked these guys, and in a very short space of time, liked one in particular. She was also angry with herself. Tonight had somehow not gone as planned. She had allowed herself to be side tracked, and not spend time getting to know John better. Now, he was sitting in the back of the ambulance, looking after his mate, probably thinking she wasn't interested in him.

He hadn't wanted her help when she offered it, but that was maybe because he was in a bit of a panic over his mate's accident. She then scolded herself for being selfish, and not considering how serious Eddie's condition could be.

"What the bloody hell happened?" questioned a voice, which although very recognisable, seemed somewhat slurred.

She turned, and looked at Myfanwy's face, which did nothing to hide the fact she was drunk.

"Eddie knocked himself out jumping off the wall," Caron replied, not wanting to waste her energy on giving details to someone who, although was her best friend, wasn't in any state to take it all in anyway. Besides she was feeling angry, and her best mate wasn't supposed to be drunk at times like this.

"I think I'm going home now," she told Myfanwy, and started to make her way down the steps to the road.

After only a few seconds Myfanwy was following her.

"Wait for me, then," she said as she carefully negotiated the steps. Caron turned, partly to make sure she made it down the steps, but also to let her know that she would be fine going down the road on her own, and that there was no reason why Myfanwy should leave too.

"It's boring anyway," Myfanwy justified. "So I'm coming too, and you can tell me why you are a bit moody." Myfanwy was slurring her words, and Caron was caught between not wanting to talk to her, because she was drunk, and wanting to talk to her because she always did. Myfanwy was good at putting a different perspective on whatever it was Caron was trying to work out.

However, on this occasion she thought it best to keep her thoughts to herself.

"I'm just tired, and it's horrible when accidents happen. I just want to go to bed now." Caron knew it wasn't very convincing, but it would have to do. Myfanwy persisted for a while, but Caron stuck to her guns, and as they reached her house, Caron gave Myfanwy a kiss on the cheek, a hug, and turned to put the key in the door.

"I'll see you tomorrow. Goodnight," she said, glanced briefly at Myfanwy, and closed the door behind her.

Myfanwy said "Goodnight" as the door closed and stood there for a few seconds longer.

"Oh my God," she whispered to herself. "She's bloody well falling for the man." She turned, a little bit too quickly for the amount she had had to drink. Losing her balance, she grasped at the gate post, as she fell, but disappeared into the small hedge outside Caron's house with a, muffled yelp.

Caron put the kettle on and then sat at the kitchen table. She heard a noise outside, but thought it must be others coming home from the party, so didn't pay it any attention. Then there was a knock at the front door.

"I could murder a cup of coffee," Myfanwy exclaimed, as Caron opened the door to see a somewhat more dishevelled best friend than she had left only a few moments ago. Myfanwy turned and looked at the hedge. "How long have you had that?" She nodded towards it. "I don't remember that being in the middle of the pathway before."

Caron smiled, gave Myfanwy a brief glance, beckoned her in, turned and walked down towards the kitchen. She was pleased Myfanwy hadn't gone home, and she wasn't that drunk, just a little 'wobbly'.

They talked for hours, as they usually did. They had a laugh, and Myfanwy did get the subject around to John, although Caron had tried her best to avoid it. There was an admission of liking him very much, but Myfanwy did reiterate the point that she had only known him for "five minutes". Caron also detected a slight softening of her ways when Myfanwy spoke about Morris, but she chose not to challenge her on it, because it would be pointless. Myfanwy would deny it anyway, even though Caron knew it was true.

So engrossed were they, time simply passed them by. Eventually, they realised it was light outside, in fact the sun was shining brightly. Another sleepless night had passed them by. Caron looked at the clock on the wall. Six forty-five.

"Well, I'd better go," Myfanwy said, as she rose from her chair.

Caron followed her to the door. Although tired, she was in a much better mood, and that was why Myfanwy was her best friend. She had this great knack of making everything seem okay.

CHAPTER NINE

At 7.45am, in the hospital, everything certainly wasn't okay. John's eyes opened sharply. It was light, but that was a little confusing. It seemed like he had only just closed his eyes. A glance up at the clock, however, told him all was not right. He sat upright, and the pain in his neck took hold for a few minutes whilst he moved his head round in a circular motion. Lying on a sofa half his length wasn't without its problems, even when it was only for a few hours.

Where was Gareth? Where was Martin? It was worrying that no one had come to take him back to Dale.

He put on his shoes, stood up and stretched. His neck and back were sore, due to the sleeping arrangements, but he needed to find Gareth. He walked out of the porter's room, but his first decision was which way to go. He chose left, as he remembered turning right into the room when Martin took him there. It was a few minutes before he came across anyone. A cleaner mopping the corridor floor.

"Do you know Martin, or Gareth?" he asked.

The cleaner looked up, he didn't look the happiest in the world at his job, but that belied his happy reply, "Gareth's finished his shift and gone home about ten minutes ago, but Martin's still here. If you follow this corridor to the end, he'll be in the canteen just on the right."

"Thanks," John replied as he hurriedly made his way towards the canteen. Surely Gareth hadn't, in fact gone home. Perhaps the cleaner just assumed he was going, as he had finished. He didn't know Gareth was going to take him back to Dale. His fast walk turned into a jog. Surely Gareth had not gone without him? He knew deep down that Gareth had probably already left, and he was going to find himself stranded once again.

The look on Martin's face when John walked through the canteen entrance said everything that John needed to know. John was 'at him' before he had chance to say anything.

"Where is he?" he asked, knowing the reply he was about to hear.

"Has he not come to tell you he's off, yet?" Martin knew this sounded weak. He knew Gareth had gone. Obviously, he had forgotten all about John because it was about twenty minutes ago he saw Gareth leaving, and he had to be honest with himself, it had also slipped his own mind that Gareth should have been going to collect John first. But he wasn't going to tell John that part. John put his forehead against the canteen door, and closed his eyes.

That's what you get for relying on brainless idiots, he thought to himself.

He looked back up, in Martin's direction.

"Taxi, bus, what's nearest?"

"You could get the ninety-seven from just around the corner. I think that goes to Dale."

"Thanks." John turned and walked back down the corridor. He would check the situation with Eddie, then get back to the others, and if they were in any fit state, tell them what happened.

As John walked into the ward, Eddie was sitting up in bed, and as soon as he saw John he started to laugh. John couldn't help but smile back although he wasn't really in the greatest mood.

"And for my next trick," Eddie said through his laughter, holding up his right arm, which was in plaster up to the elbow.

"Twat," John said, as he sat on the edge of the bed. Eddie was still laughing.

"But as long as you are okay. They want to keep you here for a while longer, because they are under the misapprehension there's a brain in there that you might have damaged." John's eyes were pointing to Eddie's head. "I'm pissing off back to find the other two who could be anywhere given the state they were in when we left."

Eddie's face looked serious, "I know, why? What are they not telling me?"

John got up and walked towards the door, and without turning back towards Eddie, he answered, "Only that you're a twat. See you later." John didn't wait for any response from Eddie, because he knew there would be questions like How do I get back? John didn't care, he'd work it out, eventually.

As luck would have it, John walked around the corner, and there was a bus with '97' on the front, so he hurried to the doors. As he stepped up to the driver, he asked how much it was to Dale.

"I don't go to Dale," the driver said.

"Fantastic!" John exclaimed. "Can this actually get any better?" Now he wasn't happy.

"Are you staying on, or getting off?" came the unsympathetic response from the driver.

John looked down the bus. He looked back at the driver. "But there's no bugger on it," he said frustrated.

"I still got to leave; there'll be folks waiting on the route."

"How close do you get to Dale?"

"About five miles, but there's a bus that goes from that village to Dale. Takes some the old dears there, and to a couple of other places. They'll let you jump on that probably."

John couldn't be bothered to discuss the matter any further. The driver told him the fare, and John paid it, requesting a 'shout' when they were at the point where he needed to get off. He sat in the seat adjacent to the driver. This morning he had lost his faith in mankind to do right by him, so if he remained in the driver's face, he couldn't forget to tell him.

After about twenty-five minutes, as the bus pulled up at a stop alongside a row of houses, rather than a village, the driver turned to John.

"Here you go, mate. If you go and knock at number four, Janice or Brian will be there. Well if Brian isn't, and I gotta say I can't see the bus, then he may have already gone." The driver was looking out across the road presumably in the direction of Janice and Brian's house.

John was stunned into silence.

"He may have already gone?" John questioned back in a frustrated tone.

The driver was still looking across the road, but appeared to be looking up and down it.

"I don't see the bus. Which is strange, so maybe he had to go early."

John walked off the bus in total disbelief.

"Has the whole world gone fuckin' mad overnight?" he said in a totally bemused, and angry voice. His volume increased towards the end of the question, but was virtually drowned out by the bus pulling off. He stood and looked at the house across the road. The one he thought the driver was looking at, and was presumably number four.

Without taking his eyes off it, he crossed the road and walked up the drive. He pressed the doorbell and waited. He guessed Janice and Brian would be no spring chickens themselves as the bungalow had an immaculate front garden, and was in full bloom. In John's mind that was an old person's home.

It became apparent he was probably never going to find out anyway, because nobody answered the door. After peering through the front bay window, just in case they were deaf as a post, but seeing no one, John walked back to the road. *Now which way?* He walked to the end of the road that the bus approached from. To the left he saw another junction with what looked like a sign post. He walked a couple of hundred yards until the information on it became readable. If John thought things had gone badly already this morning, they were just about to get a whole lot worse – 'Dale 7' it was showing.

"Fuckin' seven!" John shouted in disbelief. "You're kidding me!" There were about three houses within earshot of his outburst, but he didn't care. In fact, he didn't care about anything anymore, as he was so unbelievably pissed off with the whole thing. He continued to talk out loud to himself.

"Well, let's look at the choices. Walk fuckin' seven miles…" He paused and looked around, then started to walk in the direction of Dale. "Or walk fuckin' seven fuckin' miles!" It was just after nine o'clock, and with the sun in full view, it was starting to warm up. A very warm day was in store.

"Fuck me!" he shouted in an attempt to release some of his extreme frustration. But it didn't.

John was not happy. He checked his mobile phone, but still no signal. Everything just served to make him angrier, but he decided there was no point being bad tempered. This was going to take a long time, so it was best to try and keep his spirits up.

Two and a half hours later, and a couple of wrong turns, caused by confusing signposts, John arrived in Dale, very hot. He had failed miserably to keep those spirits up. What he needed now, was to grab his stuff from the tent, and go take a shower. That was, of course, after he had checked on Morris and Gary. Who knows what state they ended up in last night, and would they even remember what happened to him and Eddie?

He made his way up to their tents. As he approached, there was very little sign of life. He went to the one Eddie shared with Gary, opened the zip and peered in. There was Gary with his eyes closed and mouth slightly open, and most definitely not showing any signs of concern for his or Eddie's whereabouts. John looked in on his tent, and the same could be said for Morris. He lifted the flap, put his left leg in, and booted Morris.

"Wake up, fucker. I hope your head hurts!"

Morris hardly moved, but the pain now searing up the back of his left leg, made him grab it with his right hand. He opened his eyes and looked at John.

"Fuck, man, that hurt," he moaned. He didn't really know who he was talking to, only guessed. He leaned up on his left arm, and slowly John came into focus.

"Good," was John's reply. "If I've had the night and morning from hell, the least you can do is listen to me while I tell you about it. You might also want to know what happened to Eddie?"

Moments later, with Gary also rudely woken, the three were sitting outside the tents, with John relaying the course of events. It was of no surprise that neither Morris nor Gary had any recollection of what happened the previous evening; in fact, both sat there surprised that they managed to get back to the tents.

"So, when do you reckon they're going to let him out?" Gary asked.

"Probably sometime today, I think," John said. "Fuck, I don't really know." John looked at his watch. "Or care." Bitterness still in his voice. He was tired, hot, hungry and thirsty.

"So how will he get back?" Morris asked, as he wondered why the water he had put on the stove to make tea, didn't seem to be getting any hotter. "And now we got no gas left," he added as he was looking under the kettle.

John didn't care. He picked up his towel, wash bag, and change of clothes.

"I'm off to have a shower. Then I'm going to the pub, and I'm going to stay there until it gets dark," he said and walked off. The other two looked at each other, and soon they were in hot pursuit.

As they walked, the lighter side of the previous evening's events began to take over, and it wasn't long before Eddie was the butt of many jokes, and he was going to suffer once he returned. Broken wrist he may have, it wasn't going to stop them ripping into him, though, and they agreed that they should wait for his return, and give him everything they felt he deserved. Once they were showered, they would sit in the pub until he showed up.

Eddie had indeed been given the all clear to leave hospital by the early afternoon. It hadn't really occurred to him that getting back to Dale might not be easy. He asked the nurse what buses went there, but was told the same as

John, so it was slowly beginning to dawn on him that this could take him a while. He was already beginning to suffer the effects of having one arm in plaster, as everything he had in his trouser pockets, like cash, was of course in the right pocket, so he had to use his left hand to find out exactly what his cash position was.

"You out of here, then," came a friendly and slightly familiar voice from behind him.

Eddie turned with great expectation. He momentarily saw "a knight in shining armour" before him. He smiled,

"Gareth. Thought you had gone home?" Gareth and Eddie met as Gareth was finishing cleaning the ward floor. Eddie was awake, and they started chatting. For the entirety of their conversation, Gareth hadn't made the connection between Eddie and John.

"Well, I had, but realised that I think a mate of yours wanted a lift home, and I was supposed to take him. But I think I forgot."

Eddie never even questioned it. He saw his free ride home, and that was all he focused on. He was quite quick to see an opportunity present itself. Gareth had apparently messed up, and now it was time for him to make amends.

"Got to tell you that John, my mate, was not the happiest person in the world when he left here this morning. I think if you were to take me back, I could probably smooth things over." Eddie hesitated, waiting and looking for some sort of reaction, but even he could see there was nothing coming back the other way. "And then it would be okay," he added, however, uncertain as to whether he had got through to him.

Gareth had been staring at Eddie, and for a moment, stood there and blinked a couple of times. Eddie finished his words with a smile on his face, with belief that would 'clinch' the deal.

Gareth finally spoke, "No problem." And he put his hands in his jacket pockets.

They both stood there, as if waiting for someone to feed them their next line. Eddie was sure he had secured his lift, but Gareth seemed to be waiting for him to say something.

Eddie broke the awkward silence, "Okay. Great. Let's go then?" It was a sort of question, sort of instruction, and he moved a step sideways as if to let Gareth lead the way.

"Right, yes, I'm just out here," Gareth gestured, as he walked towards the hospital doors.

Eddie followed close behind, and the two of them climbed into a Ford Escort that Eddie hoped would make the distance they had to go. It was a red Mark 1, with many dents, the largest of which travelled the whole length of the near side two doors. It was almost as if the car had been rammed. But the door opened, Eddie climbed in and placed his feet in the foot well, alongside all the papers, empty sandwich boxes, and various other waste products. It was a lift, and he was prepared to put up with anything. The other guys were probably working out a way to get him home anyway, so he would keep trying to call John on his mobile, but the lack of signal was not helping matters. Eddie didn't want them to worry. He was on his way.

As the three sat in the pub. John had lost a little focus on the conversation. Caron, who he had thought about on a couple of occasions during his long walk, was quite obviously not working, and he began to wonder if the previous night's events, and his reaction towards her, had actually caused her to stay clear. He had considered this during the walk, talking to himself out loud as he did so. He had been annoyed that walking to the party, was just about the last he'd seen of her. So he probably did react a little childishly when she offered support before he left for the hospital. He kept reminding himself that he was here on holiday with three mates, not on a mission to improve his love life.

So, he refocused on the topic of conversation, but couldn't help but cast his eyes to the entrance, whenever the door opened. Gary and Morris knew exactly what was going on in John's mind, but chose to ignore it by just casting a glance at each other, and Gary making a slight shake of his head a very clear signal to Morris that it was best left alone.

As they approached the village, Eddie wasn't quite sure where the others would be. They probably wouldn't be at the tents, because they needed to find someone who was willing to drive to the hospital, and that couldn't be done from a farmer's field. So, after careful consideration, he decided it would be best to ask in the pub, to find out if anyone had seen them. He also felt obliged to ask Gareth if he wanted to come in for a drink, especially as he wasn't going to offer him any petrol money.

The pub door opened, and Eddie walked in. Catching sight of his camping mates, he expressed his happiness at returning.

"Hello, boys!" he exclaimed, as he walked towards them, lifting his plastered right arm almost in celebration.

They all greeted one another, and Eddie introduced Gareth to Gary and Morris. When it came to John, there was a slight pause.

"You sort of know each other," Eddie spoke with that awkward tone in his voice, as he looked first at John, then toward Gareth. Gareth held out his hand.

"Sorry, mate. I just totally forgot!" Gareth stopped the slightly awkward moment by admitting immediately that he had messed up.

John shook his hand, and with an ironic smile, he took any friction Gareth thought there might possibly be, immediately out of the moment. "No worries, man. I can't criticise anyone for forgetting stuff when I have the worst memory in the world. So, buy a round and we'll forget it." His last sentence was meant as a joke, but Gareth wasn't to know that, and for a moment he looked like he'd found a penny, and lost a tenner. Eddie gave it a few seconds to see if Gareth reacted positively, but soon realised that given his slightly nervous look, Gareth wasn't about to accommodate.

"No, it's okay." He interjected, realising that saving Gareth's embarrassment was going to be expensive. "I'll get these. Gareth may have forgotten you," his eyes diverting to John, "but he's done me a massive favour."

"Brilliant!" Morris was only concerned about the next beer, he wasn't too concerned about where it was coming from.

The lunchtime reunion turned into a whole afternoon session, with the five of them enjoying a few beers, and a considerable amount of humour, most of which was at Eddie's expense.

CHAPTER TEN

The whole afternoon session turned into early evening without any of them really noticing. That was until the bar staff started to arrive. John had put Caron to the back of his mind, but she appeared at the forefront as soon as she opened the door and walked in.

He gave her a glance, and she smiled. She walked over, and John suddenly felt that nervous schoolboy feeling again. She stood just behind him, and he looked up. Looking him straight in the eye, she said, "I take it last night's attention seeker is okay?" She glanced at Eddie, who rather proudly held his broken wrist in the air.

"Oh my God!" she exclaimed, having not seen it when she walked in. She put her hand on John's shoulder, and any problem he had with her concerning her 'disappearance' the night before, vanished in an instant. He took it as "there's feeling here", and she meant it to be taken as exactly that. If something came of it, great, she'd like to know more about him.

"You've broken it?" she was smiling as she said it, knowing that firstly, they were all drunk, and secondly, compared to what could have happened to a drunk man running off the end of a wall, Eddie was by no means seriously hurt. There was general laughter, and sarcastic comments flying around.

"Yes," Eddie answered, somewhat proudly. "And I need all the sympathy you can possibly give me."

Caron was in no doubt, "Self-inflicted, not one ounce of sympathy coming your way." And with that, she gave a small squeeze to John's shoulder, and went to report for duty.

The minute she appeared behind the bar, John offered to buy the drinks.

"Hey, you okay?" Caron asked, sympathetically. Myfanwy had put things into perspective during their chat, and she realised that John had probably not had the greatest evening, although she didn't have any idea what happened once they left in the ambulance.

"Yes, I'm fine." He paused. "Bloody tired and knackered, but fine." He gave her the short version of the night's events, and she listened sympathetically. On a couple of occasions she broke off to serve, and he took drinks to the table, but John felt they had moved on, and he felt good about life again.

So did Caron. In fact, they even arranged to talk when she finished work that evening. John slowed his drinking right down. He wanted to have a talk that he would remember in the morning.

Myfanwy also arrived during the evening. After checking Caron was okay, and avoiding a question about some grazing across her hands and neck, that Caron hadn't noticed last night when they were talking, she joined the guys. Quite quickly, Myfanwy was enjoying an evening with the lads.

It was no surprise that by closing time, there wasn't a sober person in the group. Gareth had stayed, and was obviously driving nowhere, so at one point in the evening's proceedings, Eddie had said he could crash at their tents. Gareth of course assumed that meant a legitimate campsite somewhere near the pub. He'd find out how dangerous it was to assume.

As the evening went on, Caron could see that it wouldn't be fair to take John away from all the fun they were having. She and Myfanwy would have a night cap, and she told John that perhaps they could catch up when he surfaced tomorrow. Initially, John was disappointed, thinking perhaps Caron was making excuses. However, after further thought, her warmth this evening reassured him enough to put all that to one side, and enjoy the rest of the night with his mates.

The pub did stay open for a little longer than normal hours, and eventually the four, and Gareth in tow, said their goodbyes to Myfanwy and Caron, and noisily stumbled out of the pub, to begin their journey up the road in the general direction of home. Both Caron and Myfanwy had to smile, as the last comment they heard was from Eddie.

"God, I'm plastered," he said, stumbling out of the door, with right arm aloft. That was followed by various comments from the others, such as "Funny", "Tosser", "…and a twat."

As they walked in the pleasantly warm night air, Morris told them that there was another, more interesting route they could take home. Instead of turning right at the top of the road, and following the track that they would normally take, Morris told them that they could cut across the field, which would take them to the small beach.

"It's a much better route," he added.

"How do you know?" came a drunk reply from Gary.

"I tried it the other day." No one was really sober enough to find that answer a little strange, considering they had only been here for two days.

They all had various difficulties negotiating the fence. Eddie finding it particularly difficult as having one arm in plaster seemed to him to be affecting his sense of balance. Nothing to do with being drunk of course. Climbing over four feet of fencing, with only one effective arm and copious amounts of alcohol in your system didn't earn him a maximum ten for style. Normally, you would hope to have mates who would lend a helping hand, but Eddie had no chance. Having briefly perched on the top he fell ungraciously down the other side. The others, having overcome that hurdle, were now contemplating the next challenge.

This challenge had presented itself due to what Gary had stepped in. Hugely funny for the others, it had been made worse by the fact that due to its depth, it had actually seeped into Gary's left shoe.

"Fuck! It's cow shit!" he exclaimed, as he was lifting his foot out of it. "Jesus!" The realisation of the mess, became more apparent.

There was full moonlight, so he could see the extent of what was a horrendous mess. It felt warm and the aroma made it totally unpleasant. The others momentarily celebrated the fact that it was Gary and not one of them that now had a shoe filled with a cow pat, but it was only a couple of minutes before, even in their drunken state, they realised that there wouldn't be just one solitary cow pat in the field. However, Morris decided that rather than all be scared to take another step forward, they should play the "cow pat jumping" game.

"Or we could just fuckin' turn round, get back over the fence, and walk down the road," Eddie said, as he had clambered to his feet. He was now turning back towards the fence, extremely grateful at this point that his uncontrolled fall hadn't landed him in the same mess Gary was in.

"Come on, Eddie. Don't be a boring git."

Eddie looked up at the night sky, knowing he had no choice, and then turned back towards the others. They were all looking around them; there appeared to be many darker patches on the ground. This was going to be a tough game.

"Right!" Morris was in charge.

"We're interested in the ones that have a crusty top." He approached one and lightly tapped it with the toe end of his shoe. It was firm.

"Now, this could have been here for ages. In which case, it's pretty solid all the way through. On the other hand, it may have only been a few hours. So it's crusty on top, but still a little moist in the middle." He looked up at the others. "I think the rules are familiar to you all? You only find out which it is, when you jump on it!"

There were a few exclamations, and nervous laughter. They all knew the game, just never believed one day they would actually be playing it. Gareth couldn't believe what he'd got himself into, but assumed trying to back out would be worse than actually taking part.

"It's okay. We can then all go for a paddle in the sea. Wash it off. Where's your sense of adventure, boys?"

"Fuck it, you first then," Gary, already having one foot covered, had nothing to lose, so he laid the challenge down to Morris.

Morris looked around. The moonlight allowed reasonable visibility, but even then it was difficult to make out crusty cow pats as they all had a similar dark shading at night. Morris decided to focus on a dark shade, and just run at it and jump. It was only a few yards, so he started towards it. He moved about half a yard, but hadn't seen the fresh one right in front of him. He slipped on that one, almost lost his balance, his left foot already carrying a moist offering, and as he managed to keep himself upright, he made it to his destination with a short leap into the air.

As he came to ground, on top of his selected pat, both feet travelled through the top crust with ease. They also travelled the very soft interior, with even more ease. In fact, so soft was the interior, there was a loud 'slapping' noise, as cow pooh splatted a good few feet in every direction, including up his own jeans. The others, who had wanted to get as close as they dare, to witness the first jump, made an alarming jump backwards, as they had not even considered the 'splash back' effect.

There was much laughter however, and Eddie didn't even wait to be told it was his go. He ran and jumped. Reasonable success, as it was obviously one that had been there a while. In fact, any taking it in turns, soon disappeared, as one by one the alcoholic hilarity of what they were doing, took over.

As they made their way across the field, the relative quietness of the late night, and distant sound of the small waves breaking on the shore, were broken by laughter, sounds of disgust, and victory shouts when an "old one" had been successfully jumped on. The odd shout of "Fuckin' hell" and "I swear this one's only just fallen out of a cow's arse", also rang out from the drunks' midnight playground. Morris actually left his shoe in one, and on retrieving it thought it would be a good idea to scoop some of the moist composition into his shoe, and then launch the contents at Eddie, who seemed to have adapted the knack of finding dry, hard cow pats, and in Morris's opinion it was only fair to share the muck. So aiming it at Eddie's feet, he redressed the balance despite Eddie's protests.

They reached the far side of the field, which had another fence, and then a small slope down to a beach. They all had varying amounts of cow manure on and in their shoes, jeans and, in Gary's case, his shirt. They decided, once Morris had told them they could get to the sea at the far end of the field, they could wash everything off in the sea anyway, so with that in mind, the jumping had become a little more carefree, and the 'game' lost any organisation it had.

So, five grown men, drunk, knackered, smelly, but having a ball, made their way down on to the beach, and headed for the water. It was a welcome sight, and by now the focus on running into the sea to wash off cow shit, meant no one was even considering how cold it might be. Except Eddie. He couldn't go jumping in because of his plaster, so his was a more cautious approach. But it soon hit all of them. Various loud, drunken cries of how cold the water was, reverberated around the small bay. However, no one other than Eddie really cared that much, as they all concentrated their individual efforts on removing any trace of cow muck. At one point, a brief splashing of one another with the immediate surrounding water, containing the recently removed cow muck, broke out, but the tide soon diluted the area, and everyone was clean but soaked to the skin. Eddie, having been concerned for almost the first time in his life, managed to keep away from the water antics, and was sure his plaster had survived.

Eventually they all left the water and made their way back up the beach and towards the field. Starting to feel a little cold, and wishing to dry off as soon as possible, John asked Morris the way to their tents from here.

"Easy," came the immediate reply from Morris. But nothing was easy when Morris was involved, so even through alcoholic intoxication John knew the chances were fairly high that Morris's "Easy" would be everything but.

"You see those rocks up there?" which no one could make out clearly because they were at the end of the beach, and therefore all anyone could see were outlines. But Morris continued, "We just have to climb up there a short way. Into the field there. Cross it, and we are almost back."

"Please not another field of cow shit?" Gary was almost pleading.

"I'm a bit more concerned about the climbing up rocks." John didn't give Morris time to answer Gary.

They were, however, walking in the direction Morris had indicated, and slowly forms of the rocks ahead, started to take shape.

They stood at the bottom of the 'short climb'. Morris started to make his way up the huge rocks, so as to try and avert any verbal abuse. But that didn't work.

"What the fuck are you doing?" Gary said.

"This can't be the only way of getting up to this field?" John asked.

"And how the fuck do I get up there with one hand, dickhead?" Eddie shouted.

"I'll help you." Gareth's comment was instinctive, rather than certain. "We'll get there."

Morris was making his way up the rocks, which didn't rise more than about thirty feet, but the first few were a little slippery, due to tidal reasons. However, the rest were relatively dry. He continued to climb whilst speaking.

"It won't take long, I'm nearly there now."

The others had started climbing. Eddie slipped with his second step, and this set him off again.

"I'm gonna add a broken leg to my injuries, you..." he paused whilst negotiating his next step. "And if I do, when its better, I'm gonna break yours, you moron!"

The others laughed, but conversation was muted by the fact that all five of them knew that one slip could mean Eddie wouldn't be the only one in plaster.

Morris had reached the top. As he made it up the small muddy verge between the rocks and the field fence, he looked into the field and could make out a dark shadow, about a hundred yards away.

"Oh fuckin' no," he whispered to himself. He moved right up to the fence. He couldn't put his hands on top of it because there was some rusty barbed wire running along it. But getting over the barbed wire was going to be the least of their problems.

There it was, standing with authority, in his field, he'd heard them coming, and his statue like pose issued a warning. *My field, you're not very welcome.* Or at least, that's what it looked like to Morris.

Bulls don't have favourites. Neither do they seem to care about being outnumbered. As the others arrived, already cursing and swearing about Morris's route home, and Eddie, having slipped and hit his plaster on one rock, was complaining that his wrist must have re-broken because it hurt so much. One by one they looked in the direction of Morris's fixed gaze.

"Is that what I think it is?" John was straining his eyes, but he knew he was right, he just wanted to hear Morris admit that he'd made another mistake.

"Christ!" Gareth let out a very worried exclamation.

His volume made the bull back off a couple of paces, but his stare never faltered.

Morris had to take control of the situation. This was his mess, he needed to sort it. Alcohol can have the effect of making someone feel slightly braver than they may otherwise be, and so he wasn't seeing this as a huge problem. Although everyone did seem to be sobering up relatively quickly.

"Okay, what we do is slowly walk around him, give him a wide berth, and he won't be interested."

"He looks very fuckin' interested to me," Eddie came back quickly, and with panic in his voice. He did, however, keep the volume of his panicked voice as low as he could. "And quite honestly, he can probably smell his shit on all of us, and is probably curious as to why we are challenging his territory." Eddie was genuinely concerned. "So I don't think he's gonna stand there and let all five of us just walk round him." He paused and still staring at the bull, he gestured, "Morris, after you, matey. We'll be right behind you."

There was an amused murmur from the other three, as Eddie put forward his suggestion; but underneath the light-hearted manner in which they were reacting, and alcohol rapidly wearing off, there was a realisation that this might not be the direction they wanted to continue in. But no one really knew what to do next.

"Well, we can't stand here all night," Gary concluded. "I'm fucking cold and wet, so we'd better think of something. Can't we move down the field a bit?"

Looking to their left and right, they couldn't really see far enough to make a judgement on safety of the ground under their feet, and no one fancied falling the distance they had just climbed. To the right of them there was some room. The field went towards the corner of the beach, but as far as they could make out, there was no route to safety, into another field. Exactly what was beyond the field to the right, they had no idea.

"Honestly, we'll be fine." Morris tried to reassure them. "He isn't gonna bother with us, if we don't bother him."

With this, Morris started to find a way of getting over the fence, and moving the rusty barbed wire at the same time. His movements were very slow and deliberate, but made very difficult by the fact that he didn't want to take his eyes off the bull, either.

"You can't be serious?" Gareth was now petrified. "Why don't we just go back down through the field and back to the road?" he almost pleaded.

"Because, this is quicker," Morris insisted, as he put his first leg over.

The barbed wire was carefully held by them all in turn, as each one made his way over the fence. They were scared, but it was funny in a strange way, with whispers of "I can't believe I'm doing this" coming from a couple of them. Each time the bull made a slight move, or noise, all five stood like statues, as if the music had stopped in a party game. Any speech was at a whisper, and once all were over, they stood inside the field afraid to be the next to move.

"We should split up and take him on both sides," Morris suggested. "That way, he'll be confused."

"Get angry, and run at one of us!" Gary interrupted.

"No, he won't. I promise you." Morris whispered, trying to reassure them as best he could. He continued, still with his eyes firmly fixed on the bull. "Someone come with me, and we'll go over to the right. The other three go left. We walk slowly, and keep watching him, don't turn away from him, and watch for cow shit… or bull shit."

"There's some. Just come out your mouth," Gary whispered, firmly.

Eddie was quick to volunteer going with Morris. Somehow it made him feel safer, although Gary pointing out that it was Morris who got them into this mess in the first place, did cause Morris to go on the defensive.

"I know what to do here,' Morris said. "If we do it this way, everything will be fine."

"Oh the irony," Gary said. "Watch for bull shit," he repeated.

John, Gary and Gareth were less convinced about being 'fine', but what choice did they have. As the three of them started to make their way forward and off to the left, Gary had made his mind up.

"We go way left." He emphasised the word 'way', so as to make it clear to John and Gareth that he meant a long way left. Neither John nor Gareth were going to argue with that, and they set out virtually parallel to the fence, not making one step towards the bull.

Morris and Eddie were a little bolder, and set out at about a 45 degree angle to the fence. All five did have one thing in common—survival.

At first the bull didn't seem concerned about what was going on. In fact, he couldn't really tell. He was just aware of movement, and he was making sure it wasn't danger. As long as this 'disturbance' kept its distance, he wasn't going to be concerned, just watchful.

However, now there was something possibly threatening. The disturbance had split into two, and appeared to be both sides of him. He had to move back, to try and keep control of the situation. So with a loud snort, he half-turned, and took a few paces backwards.

"Fuck!" Eddie shouted, and started to run. "He's comin'!"

Morris stood there in shock. He couldn't believe what Eddie was doing. He didn't want to shout, and therefore his whispered call of "Eddie" had no effect whatsoever.

Eddie was so focused on the bull, and saving his own life, he didn't see the scattered cow pats which were in his path. Cow pats that were relatively 'fresh'. Running straight into one, caused his foot to disappear from under him, and the next he knew he was lying flat on his back, with his back and head resting in warm, moist underlay. His right arm raised in the air.

There was a moment of silence and stillness. Eddie's first concern was where the bull was. He saw its big shadow, created by the moonlight, start to move towards him, and he needed to get away. Now, lying on the ground, undoubtedly in the bull's muck, he would certainly smell like one of them, if he hadn't before. He quickly turned his head and tried to lift himself up on his left side in order to find out if the bull was coming towards him, but it seemed to be motionless.

"Are you okay?" Morris whispered.

"Covered in his shit," came the reply.

Morris was soon standing by Eddie, and offering to pull him up.

"Oh, man, there's a pool of his piss over there," Morris said. "You should go and wash that shit off in it."

"You're funny." Eddie was lightly touching the back of his head whilst he replied. He could feel it was damp, and decided to just leave it. What could he do now? The priority had to be to get away from here.

With eyes on the bull, he turned to Morris, "Let's just get out of here." He'd actually had enough for once. The last twenty-four hours hadn't been the best of his life. He had managed to keep sea water and cow muck out of his plaster. He didn't know what he would have done if any amount of cow pat had slipped down between skin and plaster.

Morris replied with authority, "This time don't run off, dickhead."

With that, he pulled at Eddie's 'good' arm, and they started to make for safety again.

John, Gary and Gareth had seen their chance, and whilst the bull's focus was on Eddie and Morris's antics, they changed their direction, and took a more direct route to the far side of the field. With only minor route diversions for cow pats, they made it to the other side unscathed. Then they heard the shout.

The bull couldn't really see what was going on, he just knew something was invading his space and his field. The smell, however, was very familiar, and after hearing more noise, he decided whatever was causing it should either be warned off or attacked. So having moved back a few paces, it was time to move towards whatever it was. He had to show authority, though, so that meant a charge. He had prepared himself by focusing exactly on where the noise was coming from, and turning towards it he began his charge.

They both heard the sound of rushing hooves and snorting, and both saw the shadow moving towards them. To Eddie, suddenly the words "Don't run off" meant nothing.

"Fuckin' hell!" Eddie shouted so loud, at that time of night it could probably have been heard back in the village.

"Eddie!" Morris tried to maintain some composure.

But Eddie wasn't about to wait for any orders from Morris. He didn't wait to see if Morris even knew what was happening. He ran as fast as he could, which wasn't that quick due to being hampered by frequent slips on moist surfaces in search of safety. Morris tried to stay calm as long as he could, but even he was becoming a little unnerved when the 'shadow' and noise, was actually coming closer.

"Oh fuck," he said to himself, and was soon following Eddie as fast as his legs and underfoot conditions would allow him. He had the sense to run a slightly different course to Eddie in an attempt to confuse the bull. But neither he nor Eddie were about to stop and find out if he was still in pursuit.

Eddie reached the fence, and fortunately there was no barbed wire topping. He couldn't scramble over it quick enough, and with one arm in plaster, it proved difficult. He wasn't to know that the bull had actually given up well before he'd reached the fence. Falling to the ground on the other side, he closed his eyes, and although out of breath, relief overtook him.

Morris, with his slight detour, took a little longer to reach the fence, but reached it and cleared it with unbelievable speed. He put his hands on his knees and in the stooped position, he caught his breath back. After a few moments he looked up and started to walk towards where the others had now congregated. Glancing over the fence it took him a few seconds to find the outline of the bull, and noted that he wasn't very near to the fence. Morris reached the others; it wasn't difficult to find them as John, Gary and Gareth were having a laugh at Eddie's expense. They had watched him and Morris "leg it" over the fence, even though the bull had taken a dash at them, and stopped within a few seconds. Also, Eddie was practically covered from head to toe in cow manure, and there wasn't an immediate solution as to how he would clean himself up.

"You're sleeping in the bloody field." Gary's tone didn't leave any room for flexibility, although he did offer a solution. "Or go back and wash it all off in the sea."

"Yeah, it's only a few minutes across the field and back down those rocks," John added. "Your mate won't mind." He glanced in the direction of the field, and its occupant.

"Right." Eddie had resigned himself to the fact he was going to be 'ribbed' for the remainder of the journey, and probably into tomorrow.

"Bollocks to all of you, and let's go shall we? A shower in the morning will be fine."

"And you think the yacht club will let you in looking and smelling like that?" Morris questioned.

"Listen, we all slightly stink, so it'll be the same for you. We'll get in somehow." Eddie was trying to make it everyone's problem, not just his.

They made their way back to the tents, and the whole experience was now quite funny. Gary went inside their tent and fumbled around for a moment. He gathered up Eddie's sleeping bag, and threw it out to him with his final words on the matter.

"Stay out there you smelly git." He switched the torch off on his phone, and crashed out on his own sleeping bag.

"What would I do if it was raining?" Eddie was trying to put up a defence. There was a short silence. Then a slightly muffled reply came back from Gary.

"Then you could have slept out there, and have all that shit washed off you at the same time."

John and Morris had 'fallen' into their tent, and that left Eddie and Gareth standing in the darkness with one sleeping bag, two foldable chairs, and a gas stove. Eddie stank, there was no getting away from it. Gareth sat in one of the chairs.

"I'd really appreciate it if you slept way over there somewhere. You ain't pleasant," Gareth pleaded, gesturing towards somewhere into the field.

Eddie didn't want to sleep on or in his sleeping bag, so he unzipped the tent, threw it back in, closed the zip, grabbed the other chair, and went and sat round the back of the tents. All that could be heard for a few minutes was Eddie mumbling to himself and the creaking of the two chairs as both he and Gareth had the impossible task of trying to reach some kind of comfort in them, to enable at least a modicum of sleep. Gareth gave up, and lay on the ground. Eddie did likewise, eventually, but not before throwing the chair in the direction of the hedge in frustration.

The night fell quiet, apart from the various sleeping noises of five men who, on top of copious amounts of beer, had exerted a great deal more energy than anticipated, getting home.

CHAPTER ELEVEN

"I'm going to find out, because he's acting a bit strange, and I've asked him a couple of times, but he just gives me some bullshit answer."

"I have no idea love," Myfanwy answered.

John was discussing the antics of Morris with Myfanwy. He thought she might know something because over the first week of the holiday she and Morris had become quite friendly. But it seemed as though Morris was not acting in any strange way when he was around Myfanwy. Caron and Myfanwy had become regular drinking mates, when Caron had either finished or wasn't working, and the group had become very comfortable around each other. The guys had been taking advantage of the great weather, and mostly messing about on the beach, in the sea, and of course, in the pub. They hadn't come on holiday to do anything else, so it was working out to plan, apart from the early mishap to Eddie's arm, which he had got used to and now had several obscenities and phrases written on it.

John and Caron had spent a few moments together, but John had decided after the bull incident, that they were on holiday to have good times like that. As seemingly perfect as Caron was, he was determined that the holiday would be remembered for the four of them having spent the two weeks together, not for the three of them having great memories to talk about back home, whilst he was somewhere else with Caron. He had hinted at this in their conversation, and again in her perfect manner she seemed to show complete understanding, and always spoke to John as a friend he might have known for years. This attracted him to her even more, which made it increasingly difficult not to try and seek her affection back.

Caron and Myfanwy had listened to the 'bull incident' with amusement, and joked about how 'delightful' their tents must now smell. The next morning they all eventually managed to get cleaned up. Even Gareth had a shower, with all his clothes on, and whilst still very damp, had thanked the guys for "an interesting evening", and proceeded to drive away. He promised to come back during the two weeks for a beer, but hadn't returned yet.

Morris had consistently taken some mysterious "early morning walks", on his own, and sometimes before the others were even awake. He could then be found down at the club taking a shower, or generally wandering along by the harbour. John, Eddie and Gary hadn't spoken about it in any depth, and Eddie took the view that if Morris wanted to go out the night before, have a "skin full", then walk it off early next morning, he was entitled to do that. And of course he was. The bit John didn't quite understand was the need to do it alone. He'd have suspected a secret rendezvous with Myfanwy but firstly, she was quite adamant that wasn't the case, and anyway, Morris had been doing this virtually from day one, so it couldn't be the case anyway.

John shrugged his shoulders. "I'm seeing something that isn't there, aren't I?" he concluded, but also asked the question.

"Probably," Myfanwy answered, sounding a little disinterested.

The subject had come up because John, Gary and Eddie were sitting in the pub, and once again there was no sign of Morris. He had volunteered to go and fetch supplies from the village store, like he did every time, and as on all previous occasions it took him up to a couple of hours. When the others checked the store before entering the pub, he wasn't even there. John sat back down, and Eddie made a suggestion.

"Next time, we follow him. Then we find out where he goes, and what he does."

"Okay, two things wrong with that," John was quick to point out.

"Firstly, three of us following him, it will take him about five seconds to realise we're there. And secondly, on two or three occasions he wants to be on his own. Is that a crime, and what business is it of ours?"

"Probably none of our business at all," Eddie said. "But that doesn't stop me wanting to know what he's doing. He won't tell me, I've asked him."

"What did he say? And why didn't you tell us you'd asked?" John was slightly surprised by this revelation, and wanted to know the answer Morris gave.

"Nothing. He just said he liked to walk in some of the Welsh countryside, after all it's where he's from. And I didn't tell you, because it was a boring answer."

Eddie stopped, but it was as though he were about to say something else. However, he said no more.

"Is that it? Is that all he said?" John felt there was more.

"Well, that and 'mind your own fuckin' business'!" Eddie added.

"Which surely proves he's something to hide," Gary concluded.

"Anyway, it's eleven o'clock and I need breakfast" Eddie stood up and moved towards the bar. He turned towards Caron, who watched Eddie, a little bit mystified, because the pub didn't serve breakfast, and the lunch menu didn't start until midday.

"Caron, love," he didn't mean it to sound as patronising as it did. "We need some of these shots to start the day properly." He was pointing at the bottles of liqueurs behind the bar that still remained. He had acquired the taste from a couple of nights previous, when they decided to make their way through as many bottles as they could that were behind the bar.

The conversation had started up about how often some of them were actually used. Caron had pointed to one or two of her "personal favourites", which she knew would mean they had to try them. They weren't her favourites; in fact, she had them drinking contents of bottles that may well have been past their 'Sell By' date, but she didn't check, she just knew Rhys wanted them gone. After a while they even believed her that certain ones tasted good together. Rhys made a point of thanking Caron afterwards, as he was glad to see many of the bottles finally empty. He had decided some time ago that locals, and visitors alike, would welcome variety and wider choices. After a few months it had become apparent that wasn't the case, and his experiment failed miserably. Until, of course, John, Gary, Eddie, and Morris, the unsuspecting, had walked into his pub.

"So, I see there's still some peach schnapps. Four of those please." Then Eddie remembered his manners. Looking at Caron and Myfanwy he asked, "Six, if you two girls would like to join us?"

"You must be kidding," Myfanwy replied firmly, but with a smile on her face.

"I think I'll pass on this occasion," Caron added, as she reached for the schnapps bottle. "But thanks anyway." She lined the glasses up, and started to pour.

John and Gary had reacted to Eddie's breakfast suggestion by initially rebuking it, but on the basis that it made no difference to his decision, they reluctantly accepted this was as near to bacon and eggs as they were going to get.

"Just one, though." John was trying to lay down some authority, but it didn't really carry any weight.

Caron put the bottle on the table, as she wasn't going to stand behind the bar continually pouring. The bottle was soon empty, and during it, they had devised a penalty for which Morris had to pay due to his absence at the beginning of the session, which it had already clearly turned in to.

A half pint glass was prepared with a mixture of shots. It was felt only fair that whenever he appeared, Morris would have to catch up, and in quick time.

Sure enough, Morris entered not long after the cocktail had been made for him. Despite the protest, "As well as not looking very nice, and what if it tastes like piss too?" he was forced to accept his fate, and with much jeering, down it went. Morris hung his head for a few seconds as he placed the glass back on the table.

"Now it's your round," Eddie instructed, looking at the top of Morris's head.

Morris looked up and smiled. "My pleasure." And he stood up, probably a little too quickly. The three pints he'd had prior to arriving, then the half pint 'cocktail' suddenly made a rush to his head. Stumbling over his chair, catching the leg with his left foot, caused him to fall into the wooden pillar. The chair rocked the table, which caused several glasses to topple and roll off on to the hard floor. None of them survived in one piece, and there was a considerable amount of broken glass cascaded across the floor. There was also a scattering of people, as they moved with urgency to avoid any stray pieces of glass. A few seconds of mayhem, and then ultimately, laughter.

"Who put that there?" Morris questioned, as he looked at the table, and then at the floor.

"Who put what where?" Gary was laughing at the same time.

"That bloody table leg." Morris looked towards the bar. His initial dizziness had gone, so he focused on his destination.

Caron had headed to the kitchen as there was a large amount of clearing up to be done. She wasn't going to do it alone, though.

As they wandered back from the pub, having decided that they needed to take a little time before returning for the evening, they decided to walk along the beach, only this time without a cow pat jumping contest on the way. As they crossed the field, out of the corner of his eye, Eddie caught movement on the ground. On closer inspection, he found a small, baby rabbit, which seemed to be frozen to the spot, rather than running off as Eddie expected it to. He made a gesture to the others, and as they all gathered, it was very apparent that not all was well with their furry friend. Its eyes wide open in a startled look, it made no attempt to run away.

"He's not very well," Morris said.

John looked up at him. "I tell you what, Morris, you're always just one step ahead."

Eddie reached out to try and move the petrified creature.

"Don't do that!" Gary was alarmed. "He could be flee ridden."

"Don't be ridiculous, he's just a frightened, baby rabbit..." Eddie didn't finish.

".....that would have shot off like a....." Gary was searching for an analogy, and he found one, but said it in a tone that meant he realised it was a bit obvious, so his sentence tailed off.

"....frightened baby rabbit." Gary completed his analogy. Everyone just ignored him.

Eddie continued, "We need to leave him. We don't want to frighten him to death. Probably thinks he might be dinner."

"Not likely, especially as I see blood." John was looking from another angle, and could see evidence of it on the fur of the tiny animal."

Eddie tried to move it, and obviously in a state of complete panic, the rabbit tried to make its escape but couldn't. Eddie picked it up. There was slight intakes of breath as he did so, and it was soon very evident that the defenceless creature was wounded. Eddie, showing his softer side, spoke to it.

"Now, what's been having a go at you, then?" His voice was similar to that of a father talking to his baby son. The others just looked at each other in amusement.

"How do we know it's a rabbit anyway?" John asked, to no one in particular.

Eddie, who was now stroking the shaking, tiny ball of fur, looked at John and replied, sarcastically, "Because he's got fur and big ears... and he looks like a fuckin' rabbit!"

"Could be a hare," John was quick to retort. Eddie conceded, silently.

"How do you tell the difference?" Gary asked.

"Actually, I bet it is a hare." Morris seemed quite certain all of a sudden. He continued, "It's not very old. I mean,

113

probably a couple of weeks, and if it were a rabbit, it wouldn't have fur yet, and it would not have strayed from its mother. Hares are born with fur, and virtually run off from day one. So I reckon he's run off, and something's had a go at him. Don't know why it hasn't finished him off, but poor bugger is probably just waiting to die."

The other three looked on in total amazement. For the first time ever, Morris had imparted knowledge of quite unbelievable proportions on them.

"Thank you, doctor vet bloody Morris," Eddie replied, after being speechless for a few seconds.

Nobody was in any position to argue the theory, even if there was any point in doing so.

"I reckon we take him back to the tent with us and nurse him back to health." Eddie wasn't really asking for approval, which was just as well, because he didn't get it.

"Don't be a prat." Gary seemed disturbed by the suggestion. "The best thing we can probably do for him is put him out of his misery."

After a few minutes deliberation, during which it was established that no one would be able to "put it out of its misery", Morris took out the full box of family tissues from the bag of supplies he was carrying, and started to construct a make-shift bed for it. Taking all the tissues out and putting a few back as the base, he then packed tissues into either end, leaving a small space by the opening, which was the perfect size for a baby hare.

As Eddie was carefully placing the hare into the tissue box, talking to it as he did so, Morris had a thought.

"We should really give it a name."

"Yep, thought of that." Eddie was slowly letting go, and leaving the hare resting in the box.

"He's a hare right?" he wasn't waiting for an answer. "So 'Pubes' is appropriate."

Smiles all round, no one could argue with that.

Four grown men, slightly under the influence, and a very ill hare, now christened 'Pubes', made their way back to base.

Eddie was carrying the adopted pet, and regularly checked on its condition. With eyes still open there was a chance Pubes would pull through. As they arrived back, it was time to sleep off the excess alcohol, before venturing back to the village and taking up their residency in the pub. After Eddie's claims that Pubes was likely to be eaten by something if he was left outside the tent, Gary insisted that he be kept by the door to the tent in case "he dies and starts to smell while I'm asleep".

After a few more minutes the mini campsite—in the corner of some unsuspecting farmer's field—fell silent apart from the sound of a small winged plane passing overhead. In fact, it passed over several times, but no one was aware of it.

CHAPTER TWELVE

As the light faded, John was the first to clamber out of the tent. He was slightly disturbed by a dream he'd had, and the only bit he could remember was having a huge argument with Jo. He'd done quite well to put all of that to the back of his mind during the last few days. It came to the fore every now and then, and he had had a brief conversation with Caron, without telling her all the intimate details, and that helped. Caron didn't try to make excuses for someone she didn't know, or criticise him for overreacting. In fact, she just listened, and the small amount she did say, seemed to be reassuring.

"You should be a bloody councillor," he'd said, as their conversation ended.

Caron replied with a purposely drawn out "No..." and then added with a smile,

"I just like to know everybody else's business."

So, once again, John promised himself that once back from this break, he would make everything okay with Jo. He stood up and stretched his legs by walking up and down a little. The light was fading, and glancing at his watch, John realised that they had perhaps rested longer than intended. He kicked Eddie and Gary's tent.

"Wakey, wakey. It's nearly closing time," he called out. He stuck his head back inside the tent he shared with Morris, who was already sitting up.

"Oh fuck it!" Eddie called out.

"I think he's snuffed it. My Pubes dead." He emerged from the tent, tissue box in hand.

"His eyes are closed and..." he was prodding it with his finger, "he's a little bit still."

John went over to look. He didn't really want to, but felt compelled to. The other two also surfaced, and the general consensus of opinion was that Pubes was completely dead.

Or as Morris so eloquently put it, "Pubes was probably in so much pain he died a slow horrible death. Whereas if you'd done what Gary said in the first place, he would have been in rabbit heaven ages ago, and in a less painful way."

"We should give him a proper burial; we are by the sea, so it should be a sea burial." Eddie suggested He was ignoring Morris.

Fifteen minutes later, they were walking across the sand, towards the gently lapping sea. Eddie was carrying the deceased hare, whose bed had now been transformed into his coffin by placing a few more tissues over the top of his body, completely covering him. A few stones had been placed inside at either end, to give it some weight. The box itself was on a small piece of hardboard, which they had used as a balance for the legs of the small gas stove.

As they reached the point where the small waves were breaking on to the sand, Eddie reached into his pocket and produced the lighter they had been using to light the gas stove. A "proper sea burial" meant setting fire to the coffin as it was pushed out to sea. No one was really sure why this was 'proper', and it didn't feel quite right either. But Eddie, balancing the board on his plaster, lit the surrounding tissues, and as the flames rose, he quickly gave the lighter to John, and lowered it with his left hand and pushed it out to sea. Then the waves pushed it straight back to him, engulfed the flames, and both box and tissues were never going to be lit again. There was relief. With hindsight, setting fire to Pubes, even on his burial, seemed inhumane, so no one was upset about it. Eddie moved towards the piece of hardboard.

John offered some reassurance, "We could do without the flames, anyway."

"You got to walk it out a bit further," Morris instructed.

Eddie picked it up, and almost ran it out further, and pushed it out once more. They watched as it 'sailed' out, but after a few minutes it became difficult to see in the fading light. It must have been above water for about thirty seconds, until a slightly larger wave caused the board to tip to such an angle that the tissue box slid off into the water and then it disappeared from sight.

"Fantastic effort, that," Morris commented, as they all stared out to sea. John let out a half a laugh, and turned to walk away. Morris and Gary started to follow him. Eddie stood rooted to the spot; he was some way ahead of them in the sea, which was up to his knees. Then he turned to see the others walking away.

"We can't leave Pubes in the sea!" he called out.

Without looking back, Gary called back, "Yes we can." And they kept on walking. They didn't even turn around to find out if Eddie was following them. In fact, they didn't realise he wasn't with them until they were halfway down the road to the village. Gary glanced back at one point, but couldn't even see him in the distance. He could just make out the fence that separated the road from 'cow pat' field, but there was no sign of him.

"You don't think he drowned trying to retrieve his bloody Pubes do you?" Gary was of course joking, but all three suspected Eddie had indeed stayed to search for Pubes, but all three of them suspected there was an element of truth in the retrieving part. They continued on their journey, knowing that Eddie would be along soon enough. John turned to Morris.

"All that stuff earlier, about rabbits and hares," John paused. "True or complete made up bollocks?"

"All true," Morris replied, confidently.

"Something you studied, or knowledge you picked up at the University of Life?" Gary asked, sarcastically.

"Either way, it's a bit bizarre you know that kind of thing," John said.

"Bollocks to both of you," Morris said. "When you are born in a great country like Wales, you learn things about nature, and at some point it has its uses."

"Know much about sheep?" Gary said, mockingly.

"Fuck off!" Morris exclaimed.

They arrived at the pub. It was immediately noticeable to Myfanwy, that they were a man short.

"You lost one on the way?" she joked.

"Eddie's looking for Pubes in the sea." Gary replied instantly.

That was not the answer Myfanwy was expecting. She had no reply. Caron let out an exclamation, from behind the bar, as she walked away.

Eddie didn't have the exact point of entry for the tissue box, but he thought he was close. There was obviously no help coming from the other three, so he had a feel around under the water with his one good arm, hoping to touch something resembling a wet cardboard box. It wasn't easy, because he was keeping his head and plaster above water, and he had no idea if he was close, or miles away. In the fading light, Eddie was standing fully clothed with the sea up to his knees, bending over, looking into the water. Holding his right arm up in the air, paddling the water with his left hand, and turning in a circle. A strange sight to anyone who happened to be wandering along the beach, minding their own business. The man walking his dog did stop and have a long look at the figure standing in the sea executing a semi-pirouette motion, believing he might be witnessing a strange ritual. His attention was drawn initially, because his dog took exception to Eddie's actions, and was standing at the water's edge barking in that direction. In fact, the dog was summoning up the courage to go and check this person out, and was slowly edging its way further into the sea. Eddie was caught between keeping an eye on the dog, and continuing his search.

"You alright mate?" the man called out eventually, in a broad Welsh accent.

Eddie stood up straight. "Er, yes thanks," he said, as he tried to think of an excuse. "Looking for Pubes." He waited for a response.

The dog owner was busy trying to shut his dog up, and didn't really hear the reason for this man's slightly unorthodox activity, but actually, despite asking, he wasn't really interested. He didn't seem in distress, and what folk get up to in fading light, on a deserted beach, was no concern of his. He'd come across worse. He started to walk away.

"Okay, mate," he called back, but was looking at his dog. Eventually, the dog took notice of his owner, and the two of them wandered off into the distance. The dog looked back a couple of times, but soon lost interest. There were far more interesting things to sniff and cock a leg at on the beach.

Eddie was now talking to himself, and Pubes, as he resumed his search. "Come on now, where are you for God's sake."

Something hit his leg. It startled him, as he had no idea what it could be. He didn't know what lived in these waters. His alarm, caused him to stumble backwards, and try as he did to stay up, he failed, and fell backwards. Desperately trying to keep his plaster above water, he held his arm in the air, but he went down totally out of control, and Eddie and the plaster were momentarily submerged. He shot straight back up, and as he did so, a tissue box came to the surface with him. He grabbed it. He was dripping wet, and so was his plaster, but as he cleared the water from his eyes there was only one thing he wanted to know... was Pubes still in there? There was the evidence of the attempted 'sea burial' on the box, and considering it had been in the water for a while now, it was remarkably intact. Sure enough the main content remained, and the flames had only burnt some of the tissues and a small area of the box. Eddie started to make his way to shore, pleased with himself, for recovering Pubes. He was also trying to rub his plaster dry, but on soaking wet clothing, it was proving difficult to do.

Once off the beach, he made his way on to the field. Here, he managed to dig a small hole, using his hands and a rock. Placing the same animal into the hole, and covering it back over, Eddie satisfied himself that Pubes had now been given a proper burial. "Rest in peace little fella" Eddie said quietly, and he turned to make his way back to the tent. Now it was time to get dry, and head off to the 'wake'.

As Eddie approached the 'campsite', he could see at least two figures moving around the tents. His initial reaction was that perhaps the guys were still there, and therefore he hadn't missed anything. However, the two figures were not moving like they were 'living' there, and one of them was wearing a hat. As far as Eddie could remember, no one owned a hat, so his suspicions were aroused. Now he started to get a little nervous. "Burglars" and "Shit" he whispered to himself, and as he approached the wall, he ducked down. What did he do now? He heard them talking, so listened intently.

"Well, looks like there's four of them, judging by the number of sleeping bags. And they've been here a while, if the mess is anything to go by". The man appeared to be in his fifties with a deep, broad Welsh accent. All he knew was that the voice wasn't from a young man, and it was quite agitated, almost angry sounding. The second voice was younger.

"What we gonna do, take it all with us?" Eddie was horrified. He was starting to panic.

"No, I reckon we catch 'em early in the morning. They're probably out drinking and will be sleeping it off when we come and sort them out."

The penny dropped. Eddie realised he must be listening to the owner of the field, and probably one of his staff. Eddie decided not to introduce himself, and stayed motionless below the level of the wall.

After a few moments, it seemed as though the two men were leaving, as Eddie heard a tractor start up. His panic only increased as the vehicle noise was getting louder, as it came towards him. Eddie realised it would be coming out of the gate which was to his left, and fortunately, out of sight from where he was hiding. It was the gate they used to enter in the car when they first arrived. Fortunately, Rhys had let them leave the car in the pub car park, rather than leave it in the field. Eddie's panic intensified. If they came out of the field and turned left, their lights would illuminate him, like a rabbit caught in headlights, at the side of the road. He could see the lights on the road, as the tractor approached the gateway. He had a quick look around, but it was quite dark now, and there were no obvious escape routes. The noise of the tractor was right above him. He held his breath, and in the hope that it made him invisible, he closed his eyes.

Even with them closed, he knew a bright light was heading his way. But he kept them tightly shut. The noise of the tractor, unless he was mistaken, had reached a volume that meant it was very close, and it remained constant. He feared the worst, and he was right to. He felt movement near him.

"Are you hurt or something?" a voice enquired, loud enough to overcome the rattling sounds of diesel, and tractor.

Eddie opened his eyes, looked up, and could see the silhouette of a large person, standing directly in front of the tractor lights. He strained his eyes, and was desperately trying to stand. As he did so, he attempted to explain.

"Er, no I'm fine thanks, just a bit drunk, so I went for a walk..." he wasn't allowed to finish. The figure moved even closer to him.

"You better tell your mates to be out of my field before I come and burn the tents down tomorrow. This isn't a bloody campsite, it's private property. My property. Do you understand me, young man?"

"Yes, sir, and thank you," he said sheepishly. But as the farmer turned away, Eddie couldn't help himself, and called after him. "We are only here for another few nights, perhaps we could..."

He didn't finish the sentence. The farmer had turned back and walked towards Eddie. He came very close to Eddie's face. "Just in case I haven't made myself clear, tomorrow morning I will burn those tents down, along with anything that's in them." Eddie seemed quite certain he meant it.

"This is private property, and I'll thank you to respect that, and bugger off accordingly!"

The farmer was staring at Eddie, as if waiting for a reply, so Eddie felt he had to give him one.

"That's no to us being able to stay then?"

The farmer continued to stare for a few seconds then shook his head slightly, before walking away and climbing back into his tractor.

Eddie stood for a few seconds, but didn't need to think about the situation for very long. Even he knew tomorrow would be an early start, and 'base camp' was relocating. He had better change, and get down and report to the other guys. The farmer hadn't said by what time they had to be away, but Eddie knew farmers were early risers, and he had a feeling that their eviction would be right at the top of this farmer's "To Do" list for tomorrow. He estimated the farmer would be on his way by about 6 in the morning. Not one of them knew what 6am looked like, as on average, they had only been in bed about three hours by then.

Eddie walked purposefully into the bar and sat straight down. He did a double take at Myfanwy, as she seemed to be looking at him in a strange way. The others immediately knew something was not right, as he had not immediately asked someone to buy him a beer. He also didn't respond to the jaunts of "Eddie. Pubeless!" He looked a worried man, and looking straight at John, Gary and Morris, he began.

"We have a bit of a problem," he kept his voice down, as he didn't want others to hear. The guys didn't get the chance to ask why, as Eddie quickly continued. "I got to the tents, and we were being, well, checked out." He thought he was being cryptic just in case anyone was listening.

"Checked out?" John thought he knew what it meant, but this was Eddie, and you could never be quite sure he was saying what he meant.

"Yep. Farmer, and one of his men presumably. Sussed us out. We got to be out of there. He's coming to burn the tents down in the morning." Eddie wanted to emphasise he thought the farmer meant it. "And I gotta tell you chaps, he was serious." He paused. Then added some detail, which probably wasn't necessary. "I'm sure his breath smelt a little bit like cow shit too!" But it was enough for the others to realise he got quite close to Eddie, and in a threatening way.

"Burn them down?" Gary was the first to react. "He can't do that!"

"I think you'll find he can do what he likes on his own private land," Eddie was quick to interject.

"Shit." John was more disappointed they had been found, rather than the fact that their possessions could go up in smoke. "What else did he say?"

Eddie told them what had happened. He made his part out to be a little more 'heroic' than he had actually been, but they weren't to know that, and so there was no harm in building his own part up.

"So I bet he'll be on us by about eleven tomorrow morning," Morris said. John looked at him in complete amazement. John was intrigued.

"You think a farmer gets up about eight o'clock. Has a leisurely breakfast. Takes the kids to school. Has a cup of tea, and then starts work about ten thirty, to eleven does he?" John had half a smile on his face.

"No, I never said that." Morris was defending his reasoning, but didn't get the chance to finish.

"Try five or six in the morning. Probably more realistic," John interrupted.

It was time to have another beer, and decide what to do. And where to go?

John went to the bar. Caron began to serve him. "Got a problem?" she asked. "Going well this holiday of yours," she added, sarcastically. "Four middle-aged men come away camping. One of you breaks his arm on the second night. You go jumping in cow pats. Try to rescue a baby hare, that you call 'Pubes'..." They had eventually enlightened Caron and Myfanwy, as to the meaning of 'Pubes' in this instance. She paused as she finished one pint, and started another. "And now farmer Roberts is about to burn you down, and he'll do it too!"

"Seems Eddie has met him too, and it appears we ain't very welcome on his land."

"Shaun Roberts," Caron responded. "If he says he doesn't want you there, the best thing you can do is not be there any more."

"You know where we are, I told you. You must have known whose land we were on. If he's someone who is likely to 'kill first, ask questions later', some warning would have been nice." John wasn't angry with her, but needed to make his point.

"I know, but Myfanwy and I thought it would be nicer if you met him first. Don't worry, 'his bark is worse than his bite', as they say."

"Is it really? Or are you just saying that?" asked John.

"He's okay. Doesn't mix very well, though. He comes in sometimes with a couple of his 'boys'. They stay long enough to make the lounge smell like a pig sty, then leave. It's lovely." Caron added, as she walked away.

"Sound's pleasant." John took the pints back to the table, and sat down. He was a little more relaxed now he had some local knowledge, so he shared this with the others. However, they didn't really have much choice but to move, and so it was a relatively short discussion about what they should do. The only thing they didn't know was where to move to. Morris volunteered, not unsurprisingly, to venture out to a campsite they had passed on entering the village the week before and then report back. From Caron's words, John assumed that Mr Roberts may not set fire to anything. At worse, he might demolish a few belongings, be a bit angry, and shout a lot, but hopefully, no harm would be done.

Walking back that night the four men discussed their morning strategy. They were a little more relaxed about the whole thing, and unanimous in their thoughts about the morning after when they would rise, and pack up, ready to go.

They all slept well until about 5.30 the next morning. It was John who first heard the sound of tractors approaching. He sat up sharply, and then moved towards the tent entrance, reaching for the zip. As he did so, the reality of the situation became very clear. A few seconds to gather his thoughts, and then he sprang into action. One thing was for sure, they had very little time in which to gather their things, and move. "Morris" he shouted, as he shoved him with both hands. "Get the fuck up, they're here!" Morris woke with a startled look, and began to clamber out of his sleeping bag. John hesitated before putting his head out of the tent. When he did, he looked left, and saw Eddie and Gary's tent, motionless. He looked right, and saw four huge John Deere tractors in a neat formation, heading straight for them. John turned his head, and looked straight in front, at nothing in particular, he was taking a few seconds to compute.

"Here we go," he mumbled to himself, and climbed out of the tent. He figured this was farmer Roberts, and he was coming to claim his land back. Caron had said he was harmless, didn't bother anyone, apart from the smell, and his bark was worse than his bite. There had been no indication that he was likely to turn up with four tractors, whose back wheels, at a distance, already looked bigger than the tents, and it all looked and sounded a little aggressive. John began to feel threatened.

He moved quickly to Gary and Eddie's tent. He called to them as he unzipped the front.

"Wakey, wakey, boys. Farmer Giles has come to plough his field." He couldn't keep the concern out of his voice.

He stuck his head through the tent entrance. Gary and Eddie were showing no signs of movement.

"Boys, we gotta go!" John then turned his attention to the oncoming traffic, which was now only yards away. Engines still running, they dwarfed the tents in a very threatening manner.

Presumably, it was Shaun Roberts climbing down the side of one of them. John, standing there in a T-shirt and shorts he'd slept in, stood up straight and prepared himself for a bollocking.

"Surprised you're still here." The farmer hadn't bothered to introduce himself. He just put his face about an inch from John's. John couldn't really concentrate on his words, because the smell of, well, whatever it was, was overpowering. John thought back to being on holiday with his parents, when they stayed on a farm. He and his brother had bravely told the farmer they would help clean out the pig sties. He couldn't really remember what it smelt like, all he could remember was that it had to be the worst smell in the world. He couldn't speak for heaving. The smell of this farmer's breath was approaching that.

The farmer continued, "I thought I made myself clear to your mate last night."

Again, John said nothing. The farmer didn't look like he'd finished. "We're going to wait here for ten minutes. Then anything that's on this part of my land, after that time, will be run over by me and my boys."

There was no opportunity for a reply. The farmer turned from John, and climbed back into the tractor. John looked at the men in each tractor, and four angry faces looked back at him.

By now, the other three had dragged themselves out of the tents, and were standing behind John. Not right behind him, they suddenly weren't feeling that brave.

John turned, and looked at them. "I think we better pack up and go, boys, and fairly quickly."

There was no time to go and fetch the car and load up.

"So how the fuck do we carry everything?" Morris was concerned.

"Old pig shit breath there, doesn't care where we go, he just wants us off his land. So we dump everything the other side of this wall, and then we go get the car. The road is 'ours', he can't touch us there." John's plan made sense to them all. So under the watchful eyes of four dubious looking farmer characters, John, Gary and Morris literally threw on their clothes, packed up belongings, dismantled two tents, and threw them over the wall with lightning speed. Eddie suddenly developed "painful broken arm" syndrome, and claimed he could only provide limited assistance. In truth, they probably did it all quicker without him. To add to this surreal scene of four grown men, being evicted from a field, with four farmers in four gigantic tractors ready to flatten them when time ran out, was the fact that it started to rain. No one had noticed the cloudy skies, and how they were darkening by the minute.

A few spots of rain soon turned into a steady downpour, and it wasn't long before everyone and everything was well and truly soaked. Everyone, that is, except for the farmers who, having seen most of the belongings disappear over the wall, decided that their mission was complete, turned the tractors round, and headed back from where they came. Shaun Roberts did keep a watchful eye over his shoulder, just to make sure the squatters cleared the last few items, and left the field themselves.

By now the rain was even heavier. Past caring, the four of them stood at the side of the road looking like four lost souls, whose worldly possessions had dropped out of the sky and fallen randomly around them, such was the mess. The vision of them standing in the pouring rain, gave the scene a comical look.

"Better go fetch the car then." John smiled at the others, in an ironic way. The eviction they could deal with. Getting soaked in the process was a bit more inconvenient.

"I'll come with you." Eddie thought it was preferable to simply standing in the rain for another twenty minutes. Gary and Morris seemed to accept their fate, and began trying to construct a temporary shelter from one of the tents. Everything was so wet, however, anything they pulled in an attempt to put it over themselves, also pulled more water over them too.

As John and Eddie walked away, Morris called out, "And please hurry up, I'm fucking drowning here!"

CHAPTER THIRTEEN

It had not been a good morning. However, now that the tents were occupying legal space, and wet clothes had been changed for damp ones, calm had once again been restored. Except for the weather, which continued to support the theory that it always rains in Wales. The new, official campsite was only a short walk from the village, and the pub. Due to the inclement weather, they found solace in the pub, and discussed ways they might improve their day.

"Where do you go for a night out round here?" Eddie asked Caron and Myfanwy.

Caron and Myfanwy looked at each other, and began discussing between themselves the pros and cons of several venues, in the immediate and surrounding area. There was little in the way of a full discussion, only questions like, "What is it you want to do besides drink?" Eddie's answer of "Shag women" was not meant to be heard by the girls, but Myfanwy's sharp hearing rarely missed anything, and no one ever got away with a sexist jibe.

"Eddie, ain't no woman in Wales that desperate," came the response which told Eddie he had once again fallen foul of Myfanwy's radar like hearing.

"So happens it's Caron's night off tonight, and we thought we might go into town, have something to eat, a few drinks, and see what's goin' on at the club there." Myfanwy continued, brushing Eddie's comment to one side. "We don't mind if you chaps want to join us. Eddie, perhaps we can all watch you in action when we get to the club. That's something I'd like to see."

Eddie looked for support from his fellow campers, but naturally there wasn't any. They all agreed it was a good plan, and Eddie resigned himself to the fact that he was probably going to endure a Myfanwy backlash for most of the evening. She had already dismissed it though as "lads talk". It didn't really bother her, besides, she had her focus on another target; it was time she got to know Morris a bit better.

For John and Eddie, it would be returning to the scene of some bizarre happening, which now seemed so long ago, although it was in fact, only a week since the whole drunken arm breaking fiasco. Neither of them got to see the town in which the hospital resided, and consequently, none of its drinking establishments. However, tonight they would experience the more enjoyable part of the town, and for John anyway, he stood a better chance of getting home afterwards.

Right at the start, the evening threw up its first challenge. Myfanwy called the 'local' cab firm, which wasn't really local, and actually wasn't really a bona-fide cab firm. Craig was used to running Myfanwy and Caron from one place to another. He did it because of his unconditional love for Myfanwy. This of course, was not reciprocated, but Myfanwy was clever in that she never actually spurned Craig outright, she just made the most of his generosity, for the cost of an occasional chat in the pub or request that he take her and Caron wherever they were going. Craig was blissfully ignorant of the fact that Myfanwy wasn't interested in him, so there was a chance, at least in his eyes. It wasn't that Craig was ugly, or stupid (that was constantly questioned by Caron, on account of the fact that he still thought he had "a chance" with Myfanwy, after all these years!), but was actually a pleasant thirty-five-year old man, who simply had no friends. He worked in the yacht club, as the 'Caretaker', which involved the up-keep and all general running repairs. Members also kept him busy with their demands of requirements for their boats. But he was generally happy, living in his small rented house about five miles from Dale, and considered members of the club his friends anyway.

The problem then, for Craig, was that Myfanwy needed transport for six people. Craig owned a 1985 318 BMW, which was perfectly reliable, and had only 120,000 miles on the clock, mostly due to the fact that he bought it off an old relative, and between him and his uncle, they had never taken it beyond Cardiff and back in over forty years. It could not, however, take six adults, plus the driver. Knowing that there wouldn't be a cab firm around the area, with a six-seater, was exactly why Myfanwy called Craig. Make it his problem, not hers.

"It may not be a six-seater as such." Craig sounded hesitant, "But I think I can sort it." He didn't say it convincingly, but Myfanwy was prepared to trust him, mainly because there was little or no other choice.

"Obviously, we will pay you for whatever it costs." Myfanwy felt obliged, but knew what Craig would say.

"Oh that's no bother, perhaps we can have a drink soon?"

To which she gave her standard answer, "Of course, love. I'll let you know when Caron and I next plan a little session." They never really had "a little session", they just had times when it was the two of them putting the world to rights, and she always included Caron for back up. So there was no commitment, but hopefully, transport was sorted, even if what it was, remained in question up to the time it arrived.

They met at the pub, and all that Myfanwy had told the men was that she would organise the six-seater taxi. Caron was fully aware that they may have to be flexible with the term "six seater". They had planned to meet at seven o'clock, but Morris had once again held up proceedings with one of his late afternoon disappearing acts. John, Gary and Eddie decided the time had come to confront Morris, and find out what he was up to. After discussing it for the umpteenth time, they decided someone should follow him after all. That someone, was of course John. Eddie was willing, but failed the vote of confidence from the other two, and Gary simply wasn't interested enough. To be more accurate, he was dying to know like the other two, but wasn't prepared to put himself out.

"You'll be more sensitive to the situation anyway," was Gary's justification to John.

"Sensitive to what? We don't know where he goes, or what he does, and there are some things I could think of that I wouldn't be that sensitive about." Despite John's reservations, Gary and Eddie decided unanimously, that when Morris next 'took off', John was to follow. John could hardly wait.

"Taxi's booked for eight, so you still have time for one before we leave," Myfanwy said, making her point that 7.40 was late. John apologised, and said they had encountered issues at the club, when using the showers. The others just mumbled their agreement. It was a bit weak, but it was the best he could think of. Caron looked at John and knew immediately that it was a lie. She'd question him later.

Just after 8.15, and with Myfanwy's thumb poised over 'call' on her mobile, Craig opened the door and walked into the pub with a little apprehension. Firstly, he was late, and secondly, he hadn't quite managed a six-seater, although his argument would stand up in a court of law that it would take six people. He apologised to Myfanwy and confirmed he had something to take all six, but she was more interested in introducing him to his passengers.

Introductions complete, Craig led the way. As they followed him into the car park, there was some uncertainty as to where the taxi was. There were three what you would call normal family cars: a 4x4, and an old Transit van. It began to dawn on Myfanwy that indeed, Craig had not let her down in one sense, but "six-seater" was being interpreted slightly at odds to what she imagined. The realisation hit, as Craig moved directly towards the Transit.

"You are joking!" Caron exclaimed out loud, but to no one in particular. As Craig opened the back doors, they could see just the empty rear of the van. No fixed seats, no make-shift seats, a metal floor, a couple of pieces of copper tubing, a tyre, and what looked like a roll of carpet.

"Guys in the back, ladies up front with me." Craig hardly finished the sentence before he disappeared round the side of the van, and opened his driver's door to climb in.

The six stood there, momentarily uncertain. Myfanwy and Caron just looked at each other. Myfanwy had a wry smile on her face. They both knew there had been a level of uncertainty about this plan for transport. John, Gary, Morris and Eddie approached the opened back doors with trepidation. It was quite evident as they peered inside that something lying on that floor was damp, and had been damp for some time. The doors to this van hadn't been opened very often whilst the damp thing had been in there.

"Nice bit of carpet" Eddie commented as he climbed in and moved towards it.

He touched it. Rubbed his fingers along it a few inches, and immediately smelt his fingers. The smell made him pull his head back and stare at his fingers, as if he couldn't believe they would smell that bad. His stare remained fixed on his fingers, as he described what came to mind.

"I don't know what died on this carpet, but it died a long time ago."

The other three climbed in, each one trying not to touch anything remotely connected to the van, which proved challenging, Gary's concerns about how long they were going to be stuck in the back of this van, exposed to who knows what, meant he felt compelled to ask. "Do you actually know what's living in the back here?"

Craig was slightly unsure what to say. All four rear passengers tried to keep themselves as far away from the suspected source of all things nasty. Craig knew it wasn't pleasant back there, however, the girls were his concern, the boys could put up with it, or get out, he didn't mind either way. Myfanwy decided to defend Craig. With 'tongue in cheek', she turned her head half towards the back, and over her shoulder she instructed them to stop moaning.

"Craig has gone to great trouble and personal expense to provide this transport, so the least you can do is appreciate it." Myfanwy turned back to face the front. Caron, who had insisted sitting by the door, not next to Craig, glanced at Myfanwy's face, and noticed a little smile on it. They both new it was going to be a rough ride in the back.

There was much mumbling in the back as the four tried to position themselves as far from the roll of carpet as they could, but no one was actually prepared to sit down, so they all remained sat on their haunches. As Craig started the engine, and slowly reversed, all four fell towards the back doors. Any attempt to keep from touching the floor, or carpet, failed immediately.

"Fuckin' hell. We're gonna smell like tramps by the time we get there." Gary was quite openly, not amused.

There was much shuffling around, and trying to find a stable position as the van moved forward.

Still looking straight ahead, Myfanwy inquired of the men, "Alright back there?" Asked purely to wind up the four guys in the back even more. Caron playfully tapped Myfanwy on the arm, as if to indicate she was out of order to say that, but Caron was smiling, and didn't actually need to say anything.

As the van reached about 20 mph, Craig was having problems finding third gear, and the gear crunching was so severe it drowned out the swearing and general abusive language resonating from the rear. For the four passengers in the back, this was going to be a long journey. If indeed, the journey was ever to be completed.

Less than fifteen minutes into the journey, and nowhere near their destination, the van and its occupants were clambering out on to the side of the road. The four in the back were not as angry as they might have been, given the conditions they'd endured, but even so, there was a quick realisation from everyone that with smoke pouring out from under the bonnet, their journey was at best, going to be delayed.

Craig had lifted the bonnet, and from a cloud of smoke, came an anxious voice: "Shit, flames."

Everyone moved well away from the van, as the flames became visible to them. Myfanwy was already in conversation with the emergency services.

Within minutes, there was the sound of sirens, increasing in volume, as the group started to argue amongst themselves.

"Impressive arrangements these were." John's comment in the direction of the girls, was not met with friendly banter.

"It was the best I could do, given the circumstances," Myfanwy snapped.

"And what circumstances were those?" John knew there was going to be some reference to this supposedly being a 'girlie' night out, that the men had invited themselves on, and she had tried her best to accommodate.

He wasn't wrong. Myfanwy told him exactly that, and added "You ungrateful bastards have now ruined our evening out!"

John glanced at Caron, because he thought that perhaps Myfanwy was winding him up, and he hoped she would give him some sort of 'signal' to indicate that. But she wasn't even looking at him. Caron was looking in the direction of the siren sound as they came ever nearer. She had to do that, otherwise John would see the badly suppressed smile on her face.

Everyone stood and stared as the fire was put out. Myfanwy also called for two legitimate taxis, and despite Gary, Eddie and Morris's insistence that walking into a night club smelling of burnt out car was socially acceptable, Myfanwy and Caron were insistent that they were heading back home. John tried to rescue the evening another way.

"We have time to go back, change, and I'll book two taxis to take us into town. It will still be early enough."

"I have to shower as well," Caron responded

"Me, too." Myfanwy was quick to support her.

"Let's get the cabs to take us into town. Dinner's on me. We can relax, have a few drinks, and chill. We don't need to go clubbing, but we can still have a laugh. Come on, why does this have to screw the evening up?" John was conscious that he may be sounding as if he were pleading. He hated clubs, and was prepared to buy his way out.

There was a short silence from the girls, whilst there were rumbles of approval from the men, who were ready to accept anything that meant dinner was free.

Finally, after exchanging glances with Caron, Myfanwy spoke: "Well, I was beginning to doubt my ability to make good out of a bad situation, but," she concluded, breaking into a smile, "The magic is still there. We gratefully accept your kind invitation to dinner."

John realised he'd been 'had', looked at both girls, and took it in good grace with a smile. He didn't really mind, as long as everyone was happy, and they could have a good night, then it was worth the expense. And he couldn't deny the personal satisfaction of continuing to spend the evening in Caron's company. A fact that was blindingly obvious to Myfanwy.

By 9.30, they were heading to town with renewed hope. The girls had showered and changed, and the boys were in various states of suitable attire. Morris and Eddie had changed clothing, John and Gary had also insisted on showering at the yacht club, and once on their way, everyone was positive, and looking forward to a fun evening.

When they arrived at the restaurant, which John had been recommended to by one of the yacht club members, everyone looked suitably impressed, especially Caron and Myfanwy, who knew exactly how expensive the place was.

As they arrived at their table, Myfanwy took control of the seating arrangements, and whilst ensuring she was flanked on one side by Morris, with completely obvious intent, her instructions resulted in achieving the second objective, John and Caron seated together. Everyone was content, as the menu's arrived, and drink orders were taken.

"You don't need to pay for us." Caron turned to John, with a smile. "But you did commit a bit quick. You want to be careful, I might insist next time."

"Next time," seemed to hang in the air for John to dwell on its positive suggestion, but instead of pouncing on it, and seizing the moment, John did what he always seemed to do in such circumstances, he let it go. Not that there had been many occasions for him, but John admired any man who gained courage, on hearing a comment like that, and used it to ask for a 'date'. He really liked Caron, but he was on holiday. Did he really want to get caught up in a relationship thing? The more he thought about it, and looked at Caron, the more he thought it would be nice to think '*you ain't lost it, son.*' He smiled to himself.

However, there was a fun evening to be had, and that's what mattered right now. Everyone was hungry, so menus were the focus, and for John, also the prices on the right hand side. Oh well, he could afford it, and he was already having a good evening.

There was certainly an atmosphere of great friends out for dinner, as if it was something they had been doing for years. Funny stories about the dinner date that went wrong, which turned into the worst date and then naturally evolved into what women want from a night out, compared to what men want. Obviously, there were generalisations, which developed into a light hearted "battle of the sexes".

Occasionally, individual conversations ensued, and it was on one of those occasions Morris made a comment to Myfanwy that gave her cause to think that there was more to this "care free" man than she had first thought. It was as though something troubled him; he wasn't quite at peace with the world. She tried to dig a little after he explained that whilst being on holiday with the lads here, maybe it isn't always good to "come to a place with history".

"History?" she repeated back, in the form of a question. "What history?" she went for it, but leaned towards him, and spoke softly.

Realising his slip, he tried to recover by explaining he had once visited Dale with a girl, and the relationship didn't work out. It was weak, he knew it, and so did Myfanwy. Morris was a bit of a loner, and she doubted he would still be troubled all these years later. Myfanwy 'banked' it for now, but she wasn't going to let this one go. She liked Morris. Enough to know that Morris was holding back; it was something that bothered him, and she could be his sympathetic ear. She had no idea that a conversation had taken place at exactly the same time between Caron and John, whereby Caron had returned to the subject of them turning up late that evening.

"You weren't very convincing," she stated.

"Never was any good at lying," John replied. He proceeded to explain the strange goings on with Morris, and how he had been nominated to find out what was going on. They both looked at Morris. There was a pause.

"Or you lot could just leave him alone," Caron said, with an element of sympathy in her voice.

"Yes, we could. But you know we won't."

Caron left it, unaware that she would be returned to the subject later, by Myfanwy.

With dinner finished, no one was really interested in going home, so Caron fixed it with Rhys, that they could go back to the pub and continue their evening. John paid the bill. A couple of taxis arrived, and the party headed back.

CHAPTER FOURTEEN

9.30am isn't that early to be following somebody on foot in the Welsh countryside, except when you only got to bed at 3.30am in a slightly inebriated state. John had been woken by noises outside of the tent, and on closer inspection, realised Morris was on the move.

For Morris, it was the ideal opportunity, or so he thought. For John, it was a surprise, and damned inconvenient. John quickly threw on some clothes, and quietly unzipped the tent. As he clambered out, he heard a loud whisper

"What's going on?" John looked over to the other tent, and Gary had his head poking through the front, his eyes seemingly blinded by the morning light.

"He's on the move," John whispered back. Gary was momentarily interested.

"Is he?" he whispered back.

"No, I'm just kidding. Thought I'd get up and go for a jog." John looked at Gary, who mumbled something as he put his head back into the tent, and pulled the zip up. John moved across, and re-opened the zip. He poked his head inside.

"Anyway, you two have a lie in, take it easy, and don't worry about me, or Morris come to that," John whispered, with a slightly annoyed tone. He left their tent, making sure the coast was clear, purposely leaving their tent front open in the hope that something unpleasant would walk inside and give Gary and Eddie a rude awakening at some point.

John had no previous experience of following someone, and certainly no experience of following someone when there is absolutely no one else around for the first part of 'journey'. He made an assumption that Morris was heading down to the village, so was able to let there be a sizeable distance between the two of them. Morris headed out of the village and down a small country lane. So intent on keeping tabs on him, John did not see the sign giving direction to 'St. James' Church'.

John was becoming more and more intrigued as to Morris's possible destination. He was certainly going somewhere with intent, not just randomly taking a walk. Perhaps he was meeting somebody? Myfanwy? That theory had a flaw, because Morris had started this 'disappearing' from early on, barely before they had become friendly with the girls. So that was highly unlikely. Maybe he contacted somebody he knew many years ago, before they even got here, a female, hence the secrecy? That didn't quite fit either. He was definitely interested in Myfanwy, and you wouldn't have two on the go, but perhaps his apparent interest in Myfanwy was there to keep everyone off the trail? That was too calculated, and not a trait Morris was known for. So John just kept following, and whispered to himself, "We'll soon find out. I hope this isn't just a huge embarrassing waste of time, when I could be lying in bed."

John kept himself at a distance from Morris, and used trees and bushes to remain inconspicuous. After what felt like miles, Morris turned into a churchyard. John read the sign: "Welcome to the church of St. James." This was a development John had not even remotely expected. It took him a few seconds to comprehend, and then thought *shortcut*, so continued his pursuit without much more thought. Morris disappeared down the right hand side of the church building, and John was able to speed up to the front. It was very quiet, and just the many old tombstones gave it a very typical country church look. John peered round the wall, and Morris had obviously turned around the back, so John hurried, but trying to be light-footed on the gravel path to the back.

The pathway across the rear burial ground, was empty. "Shit, where's he gone?" He hadn't come this far just to lose him, so he hurried down the pathway. He must have travelled only a few yards, when to his right, obscured slightly by a large tree, John caught sight of someone standing. He stopped, and sure enough, it was Morris. This was very strange, and slightly weird. He seemed to be looking down, as if looking at a headstone. John didn't move, he just observed. Morris didn't move for what seemed ages, but in fact after only a couple of minutes, he turned and was facing the direction of John. Around thirty yards between them, Morris called out.

"It's okay, I'm not a grave robber. Come here, I'd like you to meet a couple of people."

John momentarily looked left and right, in the vein hope that Morris wasn't talking to him, and someone else was standing close by. But John knew he was, and he immediately wondered how long Morris had known he was being followed. As John walked towards Morris, he decided to get the embarrassment out of the way early.

"How long?" he asked.

"How long what?" Morris asked back.

"How long did you know I was following you?"

Morris paused, as if to think when it could possibly have been. "Only since you left the tent."

"Oh, that's okay. I thought you heard me getting dressed too." Replied John. They were both smiling. John, because he was slightly embarrassed. Morris, because he had told himself the best time to let it be known, would be when they arrived. Make John think he had gone the whole journey undetected.

"Why didn't you say anything?" asked John

"It was fun. You thinking you're a great detective, and me knowing you're shit." Replied Morris.

John scuffed a little, but then turned to look at the headstones directly in front of them. Before he had chance to read either one, Morris's tone slightly changed, "Mum, Dad, meet John. He's one of my mates I've been telling you about." He turned his head slightly toward John. "Meet my Mum and Dad."

John looked at Morris, and then at the two headstones. He read the names. 'Bethan Evans' and 'Gwyn Evans'. Under their names, their dates. Below that, the message on each, was "Taken but never forgotten – Your loving son Morris."

Words could not describe what was now going on John's head.

"Mate, I…" but before John could say anymore, Morris filled in all the gaps.

"They never really travelled. We didn't ever go far on holiday. They only did it because my friends always talked about their holidays, and I couldn't understand why we never went on one. We weren't poor, but there wasn't much spare money, I guess. But they liked their home comforts, and didn't see any reason to travel long distances." He paused, as if uncertain about continuing. John remained silent. He didn't feel there was anything he could say.

"That was always okay with me. Dad didn't really like driving, and Mum never passed her test, so mum and I used to shit ourselves in the back, because it made Dad a nervous driver. Anyway, they decided to take themselves away for a few days, up to Fishguard of all places. I thought they would go for somewhere a bit more rural, but I think it was the fact that it's basically one road, the A40, and Dad didn't have to worry about country lanes, and all that stuff." Again, he paused.

"So they took off one Monday morning. Early. And I mean early. 5am it was. Dad's theory, no traffic to bother him. I told him to drive at a reasonable speed, like stick to the speed limits, not the usual third gear twenty miles an hour, so as not to wind up other drivers. He told me he would be fine, and that they would call when they arrived at their hotel. I told him there wouldn't be anybody up at the time they would arrive." Another pause, he was staring at their graves, and then a deep breath. "That call never came. At least, not from him it didn't." There was now a slight quiver in his voice. "We're only talking about twenty-five miles, an hour max. So, after two hours, I thought the daft buggers had forgotten to call. Another two hours, and the phone rang. I picked it up, and asked if he'd had no change for the phone box. I don't remember too much of what was said in the next few minutes, but I was assured that they would have known very little about it. Lorry blow out, coming in the opposite direction. Took them out, and from the pictures I saw, they never had a chance.

"I never told them I loved them, before they left. It was only twenty-odd miles, so no need. All I did was tell Dad not to annoy other drivers. I felt so shit about that for years. I still do, so I needed the opportunity to tell them I regretted that. It isn't fair. They never hurt anyone. Just went about their lives being kind and generous to others. Fuck me, you have to question if there's a God."

Morris fell silent, but continued to stare at the headstones. John found it all a bit too emotional. He thought back to arguments with Jo, and how, in the context of this, and life in general, most arguments are trivial. This put everything into perspective. What would you do, if something happened, like it did to Morris's parents? He didn't want to think about it anymore. He was guilty of massive 'over reactions' in his time, but so far he hadn't paid the ultimate price. *Note to self*, he thought. *No more trivial shit. It just isn't worth it*. John took a deep breath, and broke the silence.

"Look mate, I'm so sorry. I'll leave you to your thoughts, and make my way back. And I'm sorry I followed you."

Morris was quick to reply. "Mate, it's fine. I would have insisted you do the same if it had been one of the other two. Anyway, I feel strangely at ease now I've actually told somebody about it. Should have done that years ago probably."

Morris was smiling, and John decided he should perhaps show some 'normality'. "Back home to the pub then?" Part question, mostly friendly insistence. Morris agreed, and the two set off, back to their 'home'. Morris relayed one or two 'Dad driving' stories as they walked, and John liked to think that in some small way, the slightly surreal happenings of that morning had helped Morris. He had, however, seen a completely different side to him, one which, even given the circumstances, he wouldn't have thought Morris had in him.

As Morris talked, John looked at him, and found himself wondering how he himself, would have coped with such a tragedy. Then, as horrible thoughts started to creep into his mind, and he realised he wasn't listening to Morris, he gave himself a little shake of the head, to come back to reality, and focused back on the matter in hand.

"The guys are gonna wanna know what happened," John said, as they approached the pub. He thought it probably best if they just told the truth, but he wanted it to be Morris's decision. Morris didn't hesitate.

"May as well tell them. Let's get it out there, and then we can get on with doing what we came here to do. Have fun, and get pissed."

John placed his hand on Morris's back. "If that's good for you, then who am I to argue?" Although he wasn't convinced this was something the other two would be able to move on quickly from, as it was probably the last thing they were expecting. But it was better than trying to make something up, he hoped.

As far as either John or Morris could remember, they had never experienced such silence from Gary or Eddie, following the explanation of what had happened that morning, at St. James's graveyard, and the circumstances giving rise to Morris's visit.

Gary and Eddie had expected John to return on his own, with some kind of weird story about the strange goings on of their 'wandering' mate. However, the truth could not have been further away from their own version, which, due to its now complete inappropriateness, they decided to keep to themselves. So there was an uneasy silence, then both offered their sympathy and support. Morris felt a little emotional again, as he knew the offers were genuine and heartfelt. He had a warm feeling of true friendship. One he hadn't had for a long time.

"Guys, thank you," Morris said. He didn't want this to have any effect on the great time they were having, and felt he should close the subject quickly.

"I'm sorry this has put a dampener on things, and I should have said something at the beginning."

"Mate, you've got nothing to apologise for," John said. "And what we should concentrate on now is enjoying the remainder of our time here, and, Eddie, get the bloody drinks in."

Eddie didn't disappoint, but it wasn't quite what John expected. "Gladly." Eddie stood up smiling. "I fancy the barmaid anyway, so any excuse!"

John reacted with a mumbled, "Yeah, whatever."

The situation returned to normal, and whilst not completely removed from their thoughts, they all put the events of the morning to one side, and the "four blokes camping" resumed.

One thought did occur to John, however. Given the belief by most that Morris and Myfanwy had 'connected' during the course of the trip—vehemently denied by both parties, of course—it did occur to John that Myfanwy may 'need' to know the events of the morning. Myfanwy and Caron new about the strange 'disappearances', and now the truth was out, how would Morris feel about them knowing? He wanted to mention it to Morris before they arrived at the pub, but somehow making him aware he had been the subject of 'gossip', didn't seem appropriate. Now the mood had lightened somewhat, he thought he should mention it before Myfanwy arrived. Caron, on the other hand, had worked out something was going on but wasn't totally sure. She hadn't wanted to ask Eddie, because she didn't want to make out she knew anything in the first place. The pub was empty, so she could hear some of what was said, leading her to make some assumptions, but needed clarification. John would provide that very soon, wouldn't he?

John decided to approach it in a manner that didn't let on he thought Morris had feelings for Myfanwy.

"Morris, what do we tell the girls? If actually, we tell them anything? We had mentioned a couple of times that you had gone missing, though, so they are a bit intrigued."

The door opened and in walked Myfanwy. Greetings were exchanged and then she made her way to the bar. John looked at Morris and whispered, "Whatever you think, may be it can wait?"

"No, it's okay," Morris replied. "Myfanwy is going to tell Caron now."

There were a few seconds of silence, whilst John, Gary and Eddie took in what Morris had just told them. They glanced at each other, then over to Myfanwy, who was standing at the bar, talking quietly to Caron. They then turned their attention to Morris.

"Care to explain?" John inquired. Morris momentarily looked down at the table, then leaned back slightly, so as to address them collectively, rather than just look at one in particular.

"Myfanwy knew my parents." He thought he'd leave that one out there for a few seconds, before continuing. Eyes widened, but nobody said a word. Morris continued.

"I didn't know this until last night. Turns out we went to the same school, and I won't bore you with the details, but we worked out our parents attended certain events, and the other pupils my parents talked about were Myfanwy's. What a fucking small world."

"What a fucking small village," Eddie responded to Morris's suggestion that the chances were one in several million. "Twenty-five people live around here, they all catch the same bus. Not that improbable, in my book." Eddie concluded.

"Anyway, back to the relevant stuff." John gave Eddie a look, and then fixed back on Morris. "So like, this is a school reunion then? Sort of."

Morris looked over to Myfanwy, and both she and Caron were smiling back. Caron had reacted with the same degree of surprise as the men, but she had moved quickly on to the 'love' interest, or more precisely, what happens now?

Morris and Myfanwy weren't known for their romantic side by respective friends. The previous evening, the two of them had reminisced about school days, what they could

146

remember, and played the 'I wonder what happened to him/her' game. Both giving their opinions on respective pupils and teachers. Myfanwy did know a thing or two about a few who had stayed in the area, and she gave Morris updates on their current circumstances.

To those sat around Myfanwy and Morris, it did seem as though the two had known each other for years, which is why everyone assumed it was mutual affection, not that they actually knew each other from years back. Those assumptions were all the more confirmed, when neither Morris nor Myfanwy were prepared to divulge the content of their discussions.

"Well, we don't actually remember each other, as it were, but we remember some of the school, and people. Brought some of it back actually, which was sort of nice," Morris 'explained', but without explaining anything.

For the other guys, it seemed the time to move on, and as their departure back home to 'normal' life, was only a few days away, Gary had the idea of how to end the holiday with "a bang", or party, as the slightly over-dramatic term meant. He thought the best part, was his suggestion regarding the location.

"On the beach," he rather proudly announced. As the weather had been good, and apparently was to continue, the idea indeed, seemed to be a good one.

"Locals will love that." John just fired one concern across the bows. He didn't want to be negative, he thought Gary's suggestion was actually a great idea. However, the subject of the musical entertainment came up, and it was agreed that Dave must own some form of mobile music provider. He would be invited anyway, to return the favour for his party invite, but the suggestion of open air music, brought noise implications, or so John assumed.

"On the other hand, the locals didn't seem to mind the noise from that party, so what the hell, let's do it!" John solved his own issue.

They discussed the finer detail, exact location, drink, food and music, which took about ten minutes, and then they started to invite anyone they had spoken to, or walked past, in the previous week and a half. At that point, Gary thought it a matter of courtesy to try and find Dave, to secure the music, and check he was in fact up for it. Although there was little doubt Dave would be there, and the only thing they thought would stop him, was probably his own death.

Another tactical move was to invite Rhys, and that proved fruitful as he agreed to provide a barbeque. Dave was tracked down, and to cast aside any doubt as to his attendance, his reply was: "Fucking brilliant idea." And before Gary got to the subject of music, Dave continued: "Tell you what, I'll bring the music. Got my iTunes, and speakers, can reach a decent volume, too." Gary took that as noise level wasn't going to be a problem.

All set for the final night's "Farewell Party", nothing was going to prevent it from being a fantastic bit of fun to end the holiday.

CHAPTER FIFTEEN

It seemed to arrive very quickly, in some ways, but in others, the last day felt like it was the end of an era. Within such a small community, John, Morris, Eddie and Gary had become part of the daily life, and were regularly greeted by the local residents. It felt very homely. It also appeared common knowledge that tonight's party on the beach was an open invitation. After all, it was being held in a public place and locals quite often gathered on the sand, to make the most of a beautiful summer's evening, and the guys had not made any secret of it, either. To them, it also minimised the risk of disgruntled locals.

Rhys was closing the pub early evening on account that he had realised an opportunity when he saw it.

"I'm not really closing early; I'm just moving the bar to the beach... and the kitchen. Well, the barbeque at any rate."

It seemed Rhys had it all in hand, so they left him to it. Trusting all would be well on the night.

"I'm quite looking forward to it," Caron said with a smile, as she poured the lunchtime pints. It's been a while since we had one of Rhys's beach parties."

"He's had them before?" John questioned, "Were they any good?" He added.

"Well, yes. It's been a while." She hesitated, and then added: "But the last one didn't end well." Her facial expression supported the suggestion that "didn't end well" was an understatement.

John took the drinks over and then returned for the details. "Go on then, what happened?"

Caron looked at him. She knew this was probably going to worry John, or at least make him a bit nervous, but she was confident Rhys had probably learnt his lesson, and everything would be safe. The one concerning fact, to

Caron, and also Myfanwy when they discussed it, was that Rhys said at the time "Never again. You can offer me a chance to make all the money in the world, but I'm not doing it. Barbeques can fuck right off!"

"Everything was going really well," Caron began, but John interrupted. "Disasters always start with that sentence, or something very similar." He said.

"Are you going to let me tell you?" Caron snapped back in jest.

"Sorry," John faked the hurt look.

"Rhys doesn't have a lot of patience, and so when setting up, he insists on doing it himself. That way he gets it done. No one gets in his way, or tells him to do it another way. Even if the layout is wrong…" She paused. "Or unsafe," she added, in a whisper.

Rhys was around somewhere, but she wasn't quite sure where, so just in case she lowered her voice "The barbeque wasn't secured correctly, and shall we say, became unstable. We're not really sure what caused it to happen, but the front left leg collapsed, closely followed by the front right leg. Food went everywhere."

"Oh shit," John cringed and smiled at the same time. Caron was smiling

"Yes, and then there was the hot ashes and coal. As Rhys took evasive action, he shot back and hit the table he had placed behind him, containing all of the food… well, most of it. Which then ended up all over the beach, covered in sand."

John smiled. "But he was alright, though?"

Caron nodded. "His pride took the biggest knock. Most found it briefly entertaining; in fact, it was the best entertainment of the night. What followed was a Rhys tantrum, which believe me, was even funnier. I didn't know you could say 'fuck' that many times in a sentence." She smiled. "He then continued ranting the next day, when I went in to work. He swore he'd never do it again. Cost him over a thousand pounds apparently. Which I'm pretty certain he wouldn't have been insured for, as it was off the premises."

"Perhaps I'll offer to help him put the barbeque into position, and do a quick check whilst I'm about it," John suggested. It didn't really matter what Caron's reply was going to be, he would do it anyway. Caron knew that, so she just agreed.

As John walked back to his seat, he couldn't help but think about *last day, what happens now* scenario with regard to Caron. Perhaps he would get an opportunity that evening; maybe she would even come and visit. Perhaps she wouldn't. It was going to add a little nervousness to the evening, nevertheless.

By 6pm, Rhys had left his staff to manage the business in the pub, and he was in full flow, with the barbecue set up. John, true to his word, offered his services, and although Rhys had replied with a "No, I'm fine thanks", John followed him about, until there was an appropriate time to just butt in anyway.

By 7pm, those that had spent the afternoon on the beach—and those that had arrived early—were starting to form a gathering, and Dave arrived to set up the sound system. It wasn't long before the pub had officially closed and there was a great atmosphere on the beach, with music, laughter and generally the sound of people enjoying themselves.

John, Morris, Eddie, Gary, Myfanwy, Caron, and a few locals were enjoying the evening sun, with laughter and a glass or two, with music providing the final touch to a party atmosphere.

For those who don't live by the sea, the question "When does the tide come in?" rarely gets asked or considered. It is, however, something that should be in mind, especially when you are planning to be on the beach. A beach that only has one access/exit to it, and disappears, when the tide is in. No one gave it a thought. The evening was turning into a very pleasant social event, for a few locals as well as many

151

visitors. The time spent organising seemed to have ensured everything was catered for. But such was the focus on everyone enjoying the evening, no one really noticed that by 8pm, the tide had already, noticeably turned. In fact, high tide was a matter of only 2 hours away.

"So," Eddie paused for a moment. "You and Caron…?"

"None of your business," John said.

"Okay, just looking out for you."

"Yeah, right."

Eddie glanced at Gary, and shrugged his shoulders. They weren't going to find out that way, as predicted, so plan B was needed, except they didn't have one.

The one thing it did do, however, was alert John to the fact that this was their last evening, and if he wanted to pursue anything with Caron, he was running out of time. Slight churning feeling in his stomach, because he was also out of practice at this sort of thing. In fact, it never was his area of expertise. It would take him months to find the courage, to even approach the subject of 'a date', so two weeks, and now only hours left, wasn't just outside his comfort zone, it was right around the other side of the earth. Anyway, how could it work? They lived over two hundred miles apart. Unworkable, and with the fear of rejection, John decided it best not to even go there. Matter closed.

"Well, I expect you will miss this lovely little village of ours, won't you?" From behind him came a familiar, Welsh tone, the timing of which almost suggested Caron could read his thoughts. As he turned to face her, he decided that saying nothing was not the way to deal with things, but to man up and say what he had to say.

He smiled, "Actually, I will. I don't think I have ever been to a place where everyone was so friendly." Caron was already smiling. She always did, and then he couldn't help himself. "And meeting you, and Myfanwy, was quite special. You have been the perfect hosts." Internally, he cringed a little, and hoped that it didn't sound too condescending, or pathetic.

Caron appeared to ignore the reference to herself. "Well Myfanwy and Morris seem to have connected. Well, reconnected really, I suppose. So that's a good thing." Her next comment John was not expecting, and at first he thought Caron was joking. "I guess him staying for another week, came as a surprise?" Did she mean that? Was it true? *Is she thinking it might encourage John to stay longer?* The last question was more in hope, than anything else, but even so, he was confused.

Caron could tell from John's reaction, he had no idea Morris was staying. She quickly followed up, "You didn't know, did you? Oh shit, what have I done. I'm sorry, I thought he would have told you by now."

"By now? When did he decide this, and tell everyone but the people he's actually on holiday with?" He looked up and around, as if looking for someone. "I'm assuming Gary and Eddie don't know?"

He glanced at Caron, as if she was supposed to provide the answer. Caron shrugged her shoulders. "I don't know." She was angry with herself, but had naturally assumed that Morris would have told his mates. "I'm sorry. You didn't hear it from me, right?" she asked nervously.

This had gone totally wrong. She wanted to tell John how much she had enjoyed meeting him, and getting to know him a little bit, and that perhaps they could remain friends and stay in touch. She had toyed with the idea of more than that, but decided distance would never work, so 'friends' was a good compromise. Probably, it would fade over time, but she didn't want to just say "Goodbye" and that be it. Now she had sidetracked John and needed to recover it. Straight to the point, that's the only way to deal with this.

"I was thinking it would be nice for us to perhaps er, stay in touch?" There, she'd said it, but needed to give him a get-out clause, so if he didn't want to, it wouldn't be awkward. They had exchanged numbers a couple of days after Eddie's accident, because Caron offered help should they need it. John had wondered if, after that, there might be the odd text message, but none had arrived, and he wasn't going to abuse the fact he had her number. "But it's fine if you…"

"I would like that very much," John interrupted. His previous thoughts cast aside, like some irrelevant internal rambling that made no sense. And spurred on by Morris's positive actions, he continued: "In fact, I'd like it even more if I could come back very soon to see you and maybe stay here for a while. Probably not a camping holiday, though. Unfortunately I can't be as cool as Morris and stay. I have a daughter and a company to attend to, but in a short while?" There, he'd said it, but immediately felt rejection was in the air, because Caron diverted her eyes from looking straight at him.

"You know, I'm not sure that's going to work for me. I really have…" she didn't get to finish.

"No, it's fine," John interrupted again, but this time, not in a positive way. "You don't have to explain. You don't owe me an explanation. We both have other priorities. It's fine." It wasn't "fine", and he didn't know what Caron's "other priorities" were, or if she had any; but he couldn't stay in this conversation. So he made his excuses, and seeing Gary, Eddie and Morris messing about in shallow waters, he told Caron it would only be right to spend the rest of the evening with "the boys".

"Of course," Caron replied, and they walked away from each other.

As John approached his three compatriots, Eddie saw him first, and with an inquisitive tone, he asked, "Do you think the tide's coming in? Seems it was further away than this a while ago." John had no time to question Morris about the news he had just received from Caron, regarding his travel arrangements, or lack thereof.

It didn't take them long to work out that the tide was indeed coming in, and that they also had no idea how far it would come in. A quick check on where the line of 'hard' sand met soft sand, along the beach, revealed there was no 'soft' sand. They then became aware that they weren't the only ones to be discussing matters tidal. Within only a few minutes, even Rhys had decided the barbeque party might be over and the pub should reopen. Problem was, because he had set up, in the middle of the beach, rather than by the wall, time was not on his side. Rhys began to panic, as another barbequing disaster flashed before his eyes. As there were members of his staff present, he 'ordered' them to start moving everything. For the purposes of this exercise, Rhys also considered Myfanwy, John, Eddie, Gary and Morris to be 'staff'.

Thankfully, everyone's help averted the barbeque and food from floating out to sea. Dave had rescued his sound system, as he called it, and suggested he take that to the pub too. No one objected, especially Rhys, who quickly came to realise his pub was going to be full all night, and a number of his bar staff said they would work in shifts to cover the bar. He knew he had the best job in the world, and the staff to go with it.

Everyone moved to the safety of the pub, except Caron. She had discreetly made her exit, told Myfanwy she was tired, and needed an early night. Myfanwy knew that wasn't really the truth, but put it down to John leaving, and maybe that had something to do with it. So she would find out in the morning.

In all of the excitement, John hadn't actually noticed Caron had left. Not at all how he wanted that to end, but he now needed to quiz Morris. They had all sat down, including Myfanwy, which made John feel slightly awkward, but nevertheless, there was a need to know, and Morris wasn't offering any information.

"We all looking forward to the journey home tomorrow?" John waited for a response. Gary and Eddie started to talk about how they must all come back next year, how fabulous the place was, and how great the people were. Morris and Myfanwy were strangely quiet. John looked at them both.

"Shit, you know don't you?" Morris quickly interjected.

"Bloody little madam, no wonder she scarpered," Myfanwy said.

"This is not a love thing, or anything like that," Morris began.

"Certainly not. We just have loads to talk about, and he's got some time to do it now," Myfanwy concluded, gesticulating towards Morris and stating that his decision to stay was completely of his own free will.

"You snidely little bugger." Eddie was surprised, but proud of his mate at the same time. "I never saw that coming." He was nudging Morris in that suggestive way.

Gary found himself staring and smiling at the two of them. "Fuck me," he said. "Way to go, son!"

"What does that mean, exactly?" Myfanwy asked, sternly, turning her attention to Gary specifically.

Slightly intimidated, Gary replied with hesitation, "I meant, it's nice you two know each other after all these years, and sort of find each other again kind of thing."

Gary needed help. John rescued him: "I think it's a lovely thing to do; just don't understand the secrecy. But we know now, and it's all good."

"Excellent. Well I'm going to wish you three a safe journey home tomorrow, and Morris I'll talk to you after you've said your emotional farewells." Myfanwy smiled as she finished, and then stood up. The guys stood up too, and she gave each one a short hug. "And don't you fucking dare tell anyone I just did that" she warned after hugging John.

"Don't need to," he replied. "The whole bloody pub just saw you!" A few jeers went up, and Myfanwy was heard to mumble "Bollocks" as she made for the door.

"Goodnight," she called out to no one in particular, and then left to go to Caron's house. It couldn't wait until the morning. She was only a few paces away from the pub door, when it opened again, and John called to her. She turned, and stopped.

"You're probably going to see Caron now, or soon anyway, so I just wanted to explain."

"You don't have to explain anything to me. I'm sure Caron will do that." She smiled. "You guys had an attraction, but for whatever reason, and it's none of my business, it's not going to go any further. You're a lovely man, John. Don't repeat that, either, so it's all fine. I wish you well, and maybe I'll see you again someday?"

John smiled back. "You want to be careful. Under that 'hard' exterior, there's a very caring, soft centre." He suggested.

"I have my moments," Myfanwy said. "Just not generally in public."

"Will you do me one favour?" John asked.

"Go on. No promises, mind." Myfanwy replied.

"Tell Caron I'm sorry if I offended her, and if she were to reconsider us perhaps seeing each other again, she can call me, or just send a message."

Myfanwy really did like John, and if she wanted the best for Caron, it was a fair bet he was standing in front of her right now.

"Yes, I can do that," she said, and put out her hand and touched his left arm.

"Thank you. You're not so bad yourself, you know." John smiled "And I will tell people that." Emphasising the 'will' part.

He turned and walked back into the pub. Myfanwy continued on her journey. "Caron, love," she whispered to herself. "Don't let this one go."

CHAPTER SIXTEEN

Neither John, Gary, Eddie or Morris were up the next morning at anything like the time they had planned. Discussions were had, the previous evening, about making an early start home. 8am had been agreed. At 3am, however, as they left the pub, the early start was already in jeopardy. Lack of sleep would obviously be one issue, but the drivers' intake of alcohol that evening, a bigger one.

John did not feel well, and returning from the pub he was forced to make a couple of stops, due to his system simply not coping with the amount he had drunk. Only four hours sleep, was not enough time for his body to repair the damage. It had been an entertaining walk back to the camp site. They 'sang' the entire Beatles back catalogue on the way back, to varying tunes, and words, and as they arrived at the site, they were forced to continue in whispers, for fear of waking other campers.

It was safe to say, that by 8am, the four of them were fit to go nowhere very soon. So they slept a little more. Two hours later, and the few taps of rain on their tents, turned into a deluge. The forecasted storm, which none of them knew was coming, began to bare its teeth. Lightening, thunder, wind and rain descended, and their modest tents started to buckle under the enormity of the elements being thrown at them.

"I actually think we're sinking!" came a cry from Gary and Eddie's tent. The comment was barely audible outside of their own tent, but the amount of water leaking through, did suggest they might not be as wet, if they stood outside. John and Morris weren't fairing much better.

"We should just pack our stuff, and get the hell out of here," John suggested to Morris. John had agreed to drop Morris at the pub, when they left.

"What about the tents?" Morris enquired.

"Fuck the tents. Cheap crap, and what do we need them for?" John was adamant.

"Yep, good point," Morris agreed.

John then shouted to the other two. "Pack you stuff and let's get out of here. I'll open the boot. Chuck your stuff in, and let's fuck off! Ten minutes 'til we leave."

"What about the tents?" came the reply

In unison, John and Morris shouted back, "Fuck 'em!"

Despite the awkwardness of two grown men trying to pack, within the confines of a leaky tent, the plan worked quite well, and both pairs were ready to leave their tents within minutes. John, with belongings and car keys in hand, ran to the car. He opened the boot, threw his bag in, opened the driver's door, and almost fell in, such was his desperation to seek dry 'ground'. Very wet, and still feeling slightly nauseous, John now took a moment, whilst he waited for the other three to make their move. Morris was next, and arrived in the passenger seat. Gary seemed fine too, but Eddie, who was also trying to keep his plaster dry, didn't have the same success. Looking down to make sure his plaster was covered at least a little, he ran straight into one of the guide ropes, and both him, and his possessions went crashing to the ground. Very wet ground, and the result was a very muddy Eddie. Only Morris had a view of it from the car. As he saw it happen, Morris leant his head against the window, and he closed his eyes.

"Oh shit!" he exclaimed. "Eddie's hit the ground!" John turned to look over his shoulder, but couldn't see anything. Gary could, and was the first out of the car. He helped Eddie gather everything up, throw it all in the boot, which by now had taken in quite a lot of water, and they both clambered into the car. Eddie resembled a tough mudder contestant. John's initial horror of what that would do to the interior of his car, was soon taken over by laughter, as he looked Eddie up and down.

They all sat laughing for several minutes, as the rain continued to fall. The main part of the storm seemed to have passed, but the rain continued.

"We could head to the Yacht club, and at least dry off a bit," Morris said. "In fact, you could leave me there anyway. Fucked if I'm sitting in the pub like this."

"I need a bloody shower, man." Eddie sounded defeated, but was smiling as he said it. "I'm sure I can find something in my bag, that's at least dryer than what I have on, for the journey home."

They all agreed it was worth a try, and so John headed for the Yacht club.

When they arrived, though it was still raining, it had eased off, and they were able to gather their bags from the boot, then walk, rather than dash, for the club door. However, they all looked decidedly weather beaten, and this amused the few members who had already braved the elements, to reach the club. Despite this, the four of them were glad they had made the call to go via the club, and now they just needed to find drier clothes.

After about an hour, they all felt a little more comfortable, if not completely dry. Miraculously, Eddie's plaster had suffered only minor dampness, and after a prolonged blast with a hair dryer, only small cracks were visible. He'd get it checked when they were home.

They said their goodbyes to Morris. John resisted the temptation to have one last drink in the pub before leaving. "Probably tip me over the edge," was his excuse, but that wasn't really the reason. He had to stop thinking about what might have been and head home. He wanted to see Jo and deal with that emotion next. He didn't need any side tracking. His focus would now be on the trip to see her, in September. During the holiday, he had one message from Jo, stating that she had arrived safely.

"I can't wait to see you in September," he responded.

CHAPTER SEVENTEEN

It had seemed strange to be travelling home as a party of three, rather than the original four. However, Morris had arranged to meet them back home, at the pub, in a couple of weeks. John, Eddie, and Gary spent most of the journey home, reliving some of their adventures. The topic which created the most discussion, was Eddie's drunken fall at Dave's party. He had now spent almost two weeks in plaster, but it hadn't spoilt his fun, and he was quite proud of all the signatures it had accumulated, together with the various comments. From Dave's "Just need another brick in my wall", to someone's "Who's plastered?", and a couple that he would probably need to hide from his mum, "Nice stunt, clever c…!" being the most succinct. He couldn't remember who wrote this, or others, because he didn't pay attention most of the time. John suggested a marker pen to erase offending any relations, but they decided that would take the fun out of it.

"We should make this an annual event," Eddie said. "I want a chance to be normal next time."

"You mean to the same place, or pick somewhere different?" John asked.

"I'd be happy to go back; but if the majority wanted a different place, that's cool too." Replied Eddie.

"We'd need to go somewhere different." Gary made it sound like it was his condition, to signing up again. "Keep it different each time, that way we don't get bored of the same thing."

John wasn't so interested in the destination. "I don't mind where we go, but I'm getting too old for this camping lark. A nice five star hotel, with comfy bed, and good food."

"Boring twat!" came the reply from Eddie in the back, not allowing John to finish. John smiled to himself, because he knew it wouldn't go down well and he was exaggerating the point. A bed and breakfast would do, he just didn't want to sleep on the ground, in a bloody tent.

Gary was somewhere in the middle. The camping was great fun, but not something he'd want to repeat. Four guys try camping, was the first one…

"What about a motor home?" he suggested, quite pleased with himself.

"Brilliant idea!" Eddie was already convinced. "That's more comfortable." Tapped John on the shoulder, suggesting that was his objection overcome. "And we can bloody well park it anywhere for a night, and travel around a bit each day."

"But then we end up driving all day." John responded.

"No, not at all. We plan it before we leave. It will be brilliant." Eddie needed no more convincing, and was genuinely excited by the thought.

"And you're going to be okay with the cost?" was John's next question.

"I'm sure we can cover it," Eddie replied. He had no idea how much it would cost; he hadn't even thought about cost, he just wanted to do it. John wasn't actually against the idea, so he told Eddie and Gary they should talk about it more when Morris had returned.

"He'll be fuckin' married by then," Eddie stated, with certainty in his voice.

"Who to? Myfanwy?" John said with surprise in his tone. "What the hell makes you think that? Neither one of them are the marrying type. And it's not like they are shagging or anything…" John paused. "Unless you know something I don't?" he asked, looking at Eddie through the rear-view mirror.

"No, I'm just guessing. But they do quite like each other, you know. I think they might snog quite soon." All three smiled, but only one of them felt a little tinge of regret, as he thought about that scenario.

After dropping Eddie and Gary off, John drove home contemplating the last couple of weeks. It had been a great laugh, and just what he had needed, given what had happened with Jo. Two weeks of 'escapism' with those three each year, just might be the perfect release from day-to-day life. Obviously, his daughter was his number one concern, but other than that, he hadn't really thought about much during the last two weeks, and now he was even more convinced it had been a good idea. His thoughts moved to Caron, and were tinged with a little sadness, as their 'relationship', if you could call it that, had been a very natural one, and he liked her a lot. But it was a holiday 'romance', without actually being a romance, and ended rather abruptly, which was the sad part. Perhaps he should not have let it end that way, but it was done, and their brief encounter had added an extra something to the holiday, without being complicated, or taking control of it. When he looked back over the last two weeks, the outstanding memories were those that included the four guys just messing about, in a tent, in the Welsh countryside, and now it was back to reality. Good on Morris, though. There was obviously something there with Myfanwy, even if they had initially passed it off as "old school mates". Didn't matter what came out of it, the holiday had created what looked like had the makings of at least a true friendship, and possibly more. Morris's sad memories, were now hopefully, accompanied by happiness for the future.

Overall, John felt quite content as he contemplated the return to 'normal' life. He turned the final corner into his road, as the phone rang. He glanced at the screen, to determine if right now he wanted to speak to anyone.

The display read 'Caron'.

Ingram Content Group UK Ltd.
Milton Keynes UK
UKHW040843190623
423681UK00004B/237